6 Great Fiction Stories In One!

Seasons of Love to Deep South Love

A NOVEL BY
TAMARA D. BARNETT

ISBN: 978-1-961677-83-8 (Paperback)

Library of Congress Control Number: 2023916030

Printed in the United States of America

Published by:

info@thequippyquill.com
(302) 295-2278

Love for Life

Tamara D. Barnett

CONTENTS

THE FIRST Chapter
1991

It was a Thursday afternoon in Kansas City, Missouri where the atmosphere was calm and cool. "It's early fall and many college students were just getting started at Penn Valley Community College such as a nineteen-year-old female named Shonda Lloyd. "This is going to be the most wonderful weekend of my life," Shonda said. "What are you talking about?" Chanequa Blackwood asked, who was Shonda's best friend. "This Saturday is going to be me and RJ's third anniversary."

"Good for you two," Chanequa said. "I can't believe it's been that long," Shonda said. "Tell me, Shonda, what is so great about RJ?"

"Girl you just don't know. RJ is the most wonderful guy in the world."

"What makes him the most wonderful guy in the world?"

"We do everything together and spend quality time with one another."

"So, you're saying RJ has never done anything wrong like cheat on you?"

"No, not my RJ."

Chanequa looks up, shaking her head. "Lord help this child."

Shonda stares at Chanequa with a puzzled look on her face. "What?" Shonda asked. "Girl this is the nineties. There is really no good men in this world."

Shonda rolled her eyes. "You're just saying that because you keep dating the wrong type of guys. Besides RJ planned a very perfect evening for our anniversary."

Chanequa just sighed. "Well whatever you say, Shonda."

It is now 7:30 in the evening. A group of guys were in the basement of RJ Richardson's home Montrell and Pete who are brothers, Sean and RJ were all sitting at a table playing spades. "So, are we going to be hitting the clubs on Saturday night?" Montrell asked. "You don't have to ask me I'm definitely going," Sean asked. "Montrell, you need to be coughing up that money you owe me because I need to get some speakers put in my car," Pete said. "Yeah, yeah, yeah," Montrell responded. "So, are we on for Saturday?"

"Yes, you know it," Pete said. Pete, Montrell, and Sean looked at RJ because he wasn't saying anything. 'Are you going out with us Saturday, RJ?" Sean asked. "Oh me... nope I have other plans."

"I bet you it has something to do with Shonda," Sean said. "Yes, we're going out to eat down in the Plaza. We're having a fun and romantic weekend."

Montrell and the others look at each other then they look at RJ in disbelief Montrell starts shaking his head. "RJ, RJ, RJ, RJ...What's up with all this romantic stuff?"

"Do you have a problem?" RJ asked. "Look at you RJ. You use to be a man that could get all the ladies and you still can."

"I told you guys before I don't do clubs anymore."

"He don't go to clubs because his girl isn't twenty-one," Pete said. "No Shonda has him whipped," Sean said. "For you idiot's information, I stopped going to clubs because their nothing but trouble and there's nothing but horny hostile people looking to get laid. So the club scene ain't for me."

"You really have changed RJ," Montrell said. "It's called maturity. The level none of you guys have reached," RJ said. RJ looks at his watch. "Damn look at the time. It's time for you fellows to get up out of my house. I have to go to work in the mourning."

Pete stacked the cards up and they left. "RJ is tripping," Sean said, before they got in the car. "Ever since he's been hanging around Chanequa's older brother, Eugene, RJ turned mellow," Pete said. "I have a plan that will make him want to come down to club with us," Montrell said. "Ginger Anderson."

"Hot Ginger?" Sean asked. "The one woman RJ dated when he was in college. They were like sugar and spice. He craved that woman. RJ couldn't get enough of her."

"Who couldn't," Montrell said. "She was a Jasmine Guy and Halle Berry put together…and skin like brown sugar."

"I bet when he kissed her, her lips tasted like cinnamon," Pete said. "Her mama and daddy knew what they were doing when they named her Ginger."

"Why did they split up anyway?" Sean asked. "Ginger had to move away to California. She's back in town for the week and she wants to take her cousin from California, out for some fun and I told them to come down to club Bodyworks this weekend," Montrell said. "That's perfect. When RJ finds out Ginger is going to be at the club, he'll definitely come," Pete said. "Yep Ginger is his weakness," Montrell said. "RJ is a twenty-four-year-old dating a nineteen-year-old. A sad case. "Well let's do this thang," Montrell said. RJ went back upstairs to his garage. He went around his car to shut the garage door and locked it. Then he went back inside to his bedroom and laid back on his bed. RJ began to think about things. Good thoughts.

About how blessed he was to have a paid for house. His parents let him have it after he finished college because they decided to move to Atlanta. He may be the only child but the Blackwood's were his family in Kansas City Eugene Blackwood has always been a good influence on him. Eugene recently became a minister. Chanequa Blackwood has always been like a baby sister to him.

Sidney and Redmond Blackwood who were Eugene and Chanequa's parents were like his advisors. They gave great advice. His girl Shonda Lloyd was the love of his life.

They meant the world to world to each other. It was just like yesterday when they first met at Chanequa's seventeenth birthday party in 1988. Eugene chaperoned the party. RJ, Pete, Montrell, and Sean were standing against the wall watching everyone dance. "This party sucks," Pete said. "It's some cute girls here though," Montrell said.

"These girls are too young," Sean said. "Like age ever stopped you," RJ said. "I don't want to be here. I'd rather be at home with my girl," Pete said. "Then why are you here?" RJ asked. "I'm just here because of Chanequa."

Chanequa comes over to them. "Why are all of you just standing here holding up the wall?"

"Pete said your party sucks," Sean said. "Don't pay him no mind sweetheart. You're looking good in that dress" Pete said. Chanequa ignored what Pete said but focused on RJ. "There is food and drink if you ever get hungry or thirsty." She walked away to let someone in the front door.

That's when RJ saw her. Shonda following Chanequa back into the dining room carrying a pot. "You can sit it here on this table," Chanequa said. He thought she was so pretty and innocent looking but she was also too young. "What are you staring at RJ?" Sean asked. "Nothing."

"He's checking out Chanequa's friend," Montrell said. "None of you guys know what you are talking about," RJ said. "She's too young for me anyway." He still kept staring at her.

Chanequa and Shonda were fixing themselves some nachos and dip. The DJ started playing some Salt N Pepa "Push It." Everyone was having a good time. RJ and the others were still standing against the wall. "Who are those guys just standing against the wall?" Shonda asked. "The one on the left is RJ. He's a sweetie and a very close friend of the family. Them other three you don't want to know them."

Shonda was pouring some punch into a paper cup but the cup tipped over and some of the punch spilled on her skirt. "Shoot!" Shonda said. "I'm going to the bathroom to clean off. "Okay," Chanequa said. RJ came over after Shonda went to the bathroom. "So what's up RJ? You should be having some fun not hanging out with the three stooges."

"I am. This is a nice party but I gotta go."

"Why?"

"I have to get some sleep. I haven't had any lately. But I'll take some punch before I go."

RJ poured some punch in a paper cup then he drank some. He kept drinking more of it. "I got to go to the bathroom," he said after his fourth cup. He headed for the bathroom. Shonda was coming out of the bathroom. Shonda smiled at him shyly when she walked pass him. "You're Chanequa's friend?" She stopped and turned around and answered "yes."

"I'm RJ Richardson. "He held out his hand. She shook it. "I'm real close to Chanequa's whole family. Maybe we can be close, get to know each other."

"You look a little too old for me and why me?"

"I think you're cute and you seem like a nice girl. I like nice girls."

"Me you …I don't think so. "They went back to party. The DJ slowed it down with some Keith Sweat "Make It Last Forever."

"Can I dance with you?" RJ asked Shonda. "You don't give up, do you?"

"I just want to dance with you."

"It's not going to hurt to dance," Chanequa said. Shonda and RJ danced. This was actually Shonda's first time ever being this close to a guy. She must admit it was pretty nice. His arms was wrapped around her and she laid her head on his shoulder. She felt protected. Shonda and RJ walked to his car after the song ended. Pete, Montrell, and Sean were outside talking. "I knew he was going to talk to her," Pete said. "We should go out sometime," RJ said. Shonda had an unsure look on her face. "I know we have an age difference but whatever we do Chanequa can be there."

"I'll see," Shonda said. "I'll go with that," RJ said. "Have fun."

"Thanks for the dance," she said. Shonda went back inside. RJ and the fellows got into the car. "You got her number?" Sean asked. "I didn't get her number. We just talked and danced."

He started the car, then drove off. RJ and Shonda started hanging out a week after they met. They're time together was like family affairs because they spent it with the Blackwood's. They would often play cards and order pizza. After a few months of that, they spent time alone. They went out but RJ kept their relationship on low key. He brought Shonda around Pete, Sean, or Montrell. They eventually found out about them. RJ never regretted any moment of their time together. It was something unique and spiritual about their relationship. They both were experiencing what love was like. They waited a while before they gave themselves to each other. Those nights were so passionate and worthwhile.

RJ woke up. It was twelve o' clock in the mourning. He didn't know he dosed off and was still in his clothes. RJ got up and went to the bathroom to brush his teeth. Then he put on his pajamas then went back to bed. RJ just left his job at Firestone for the day. RJ and his father worked on cars back in the day when his father served in the Army. It felt good to be at home and have the weekend off. He did his everyday routine, feed Manni his female rottweiler, and then get dinner ready. He decided against cooking for tonight. RJ wanted to relax for tomorrow. He took a shower, then he got into his bathrobe. Shonda came about eight fifteen. "How was school and work today?" he asked after they shared a kiss and a hug. "I'm glad the day is over," she said. They went to the bedroom and Shonda sat her gym bag on the floor next to the bed. They sat on the bed and then started kissing. RJ paused but then asked, "You want to get some Go Chicken Go?"

"Sure, I'm hungry. Before we go I want to talk about tomorrow."

RJ laid back on the bed. "We're still going to Houlihan's on the Plaza" he said. "Afterwards I was thinking we should do something erotic, something we've never done before."

"Like what?"

"I got some video equipment. I want us to make a movie."

"You want us to make a porno?"

"No nothing too wild. Just a sexy love scene. I want us to take our relationship to another level."

Shonda laid on top of him. "So, we're going to do something real freaky?"

"I love seeing you lying in my bed with your lingerie on."

Shonda stood up. "Well you're going to have one of the best actresses you ever seen."

RJ sat up. "Baby you know what I was thinking?"

"What?"

"Getting a swimming pool put in the backyard. Have some pool parties and some private sex in the pool parties."

"But I can't swim RJ."

"You ain't gotta know how to swim. All you need is your body in your bikini."

So if I was in the middle of the ocean, drowning, would you save me?" RJ was rubbing h chin with a smirk on his face."

"I guess not."

"Yeah baby I would save you."

"You're just saying that."

"I would for real. Except if Jaws was in the water."

"You're wrong RJ."

She was hitting him because he was laughing. Then they started making out. "We have to stop. We have to save all our fun for tomorrow," Shonda said. "Damn tomorrow. Tomorrow may not come," he said. "Trust in the Lord and it shall be."

"Guess I gotta wait since you talked religion to me."

"Are we still something to eat?" She asked. Shonda and Chanequa went to the Bannister Mall on Saturday afternoon. "Victoria Secrets or Frederick Hollywood?" Shonda asked. "The choice is yours," Chanequa said. "I guess Victoria Secrets."

"While you're lingerie shopping, I'm getting myself a smoothie."

"Okay enjoy yourself," Shonda said. RJ went over to Pete and his baby mama Pashay's apartment. Pete's son was lying down on the floor putting a puzzle together. Pashay was sitting on the couch with their daughter, doing her hair. "Okay what's going on Pete?" RJ asked. "I didn't get to mention I have a cousin of mine's birthday is today and it's going to be a birthday party at Bodywork's tonight."

"Pete I told you I'm not going."

"Yeah I remember what you told me. I'm not asking you to break your plans with Shonda Just have a drink, hang out for a little bit and nothing else. Shonda won't even miss you."

"Why do you want me to go out with you guys so badly this weekend? Are you trying to hook me up with some other woman?"

"I wouldn't do that. I know how you feel about Shonda. "Okay man. One drink and I'm out."

"That's what I'm talking about. Be there about ten."

RJ nodded his head and said good-bye to Pashay and the kids. They said the same to him. RJ and Shonda ate at Houlihan's then they stopped at Shonda's place. "I'm going to pick you up later. I gotta make a quick run."

"What about our movie?" Shonda asked. "Don't worry we still have time."

She gave him a kiss. "Don't be too long." Shonda went in the house.

RJ headed to the club. He got there ten on the dot. It was already crowded. Pete was at the bar getting a beer. "Hey RJ."

"What's up man?" RJ asked. "You're right on time."

They walked over to the table where Montrell, Sean, and two women were sitting. "Hello RJ," a soft sweet sexy voice said. RJ couldn't really see the woman's face that said his name until she stood up. His mouth was wide open. "G-G-Ginger," he tried to say. "I missed you RJ." Ginger gave him a hug. "Shanese you want to dance?" Sean asked Ginger's cousin. "It's Shanelle…I guess so. "I guess we're going to find some women to dance with," Montrell said. "Yeah you two can catch up with some things," Pete said. RJ and

Ginger had the table to themselves. "Oh Ginger, I'd never thought I would see you again."

"I've always thought I'd see you again," she said. Ginger scooted closer to him. Then she tongue kissed him. RJ got hot and horny but he had to set something straight. "Ginger wait…I have a girlfriend right now."

"Oh … how come you're here without her?"

"Because she's not twenty-one."

"You're dating a kid?"

"She's not a kid. She's very mature and fun to be with that's why I'm in love with her."

"I thought…or we…could rekindle our flame."

RJ shook his head. "Please RJ."

She had her hand on his thigh with her nails sunk in it. The look on her face was so pathetic he got up to get a drink because he hated to see that look on her face. RJ drank so much that night he got drunk.

Shonda was sitting on the couch with her twin cousins, Relisha and Kelisha, watching BET music videos, eating peanuts and mints. It was almost one in morning and Shonda was very upset But she knew she had to trust him. Her cousins went to bed while she stayed up, flicking through the channels. Then she turned the TV off. Shonda got into her Toyota Corolla, heading to RJ's house Ginger drove RJ home in his car. RJ was leaning against the window. When he opened the car door, he threw up on the sidewalk. Ginger helped him in the house to his bedroom. He flopped on the bed. "Goodness RJ," she was fanning away the smell of his breath, "you had too much to drink."

"Yeah but I'm cool, I'm home. I'm going to sleep now. "Come on RJ … why don't we get the party started?" She asked, rubbing on his chest. "Ginger you need to leave."

She unbuttons his shirt. "What if I don't want to leave?" She places wet kisses on his bare chest. Shonda just now gets to RJ's house. His car was there. She didn't understand. He didn't call or nothing. Shonda has a feeling she's been stood up. She got out of the car. It was chilly out because it rained a little, earlier. Shonda knocked on the door and rang the doorbell. No one answered. She used the door key copy to let herself in. "RJ!" She called. Shonda heard talking in the bedroom. She went towards the bedroom and she saw Ginger in the bed with RJ. "What's going on here?"

"Hey Shonda baby this isn't what you think."

"Then what is she doing here?"

"I got drunk, Ginger brought me home."

Shonda didn't want to hear no more so she walked out. "Shonda!" RJ tried to go after her but he hit the floor when he got off the bed. "Damn I've got a headache," he said. Mama Sidney set the table for their family Sunday dinner after church. They were having black eyed peas, cornbread, collard greens, baked chicken, and yams. Papa Redmond was the first one seated. RJ and Eugene sat next to each other. "Eugene I'm so proud of you…preaching your first sermon," Sidney said. They all clapped. "Yeah you were amazing my man," RJ said, patting Eugene on the back. "RJ you should take part in the church," Eugene said. "Naah I don't think that's for me."

"Can we eat now?" Redmond asked. "Wait a second where's Chanequa?" Sidney asked. "Probably in her room," Eugene said. "Chanequa get your butt out here so we can eat!" Redmond yelled. Chanequa was dragging her feet to the dining room. "Sit Chanequa it's time to eat," Sidney said. "I'm not hungry."

"You're not hungry," Redmond said. "I'm on a diet."

"Girl you don't need to be on a diet," Sidney said. "Mama I'm not hungry!"

"As long as you live in this house you're going to eat. Now sit!" Chanequa sits. RJ began filling his plate up and dug right in. Everyone was staring at him. "We have to say grace first," Eugene whispered to him. "Oh, my bad." RJ put his fork down.

They all held hands and Sidney said grace. Then they all began grubbing except Chanequa was picking at her food. She looked at RJ. "So, RJ, how was you and Shonda's evening?"

"Let's talk about that later." he said. "Eat!" Redmond said. Chanequa just ate little bites at a time. That evening, Chanequa called Shonda. "Did you have fun last night?"

"At first … what happened?" I caught RJ in the bed with another woman."

"I'm lost. How was he with you but then end up in bed with another woman?"

"We went out to eat then he took me home, said he was going to be back soon, was gone for a very long time so I drove by his house, seen them two in bed."

"Wow that doesn't sound like RJ."

"They still had their clothes on but I know they were about to do something."

"That's a weird situation. You didn't ask him where he was going?"

"No I trust him. He never gave me a reason not to trust him before."

"Well maybe it's nothing."

"How can it not be? He had a woman in his bedroom."

"Have you two talked today?"

"I have nothing to say to RJ."

"Are you breaking up with him?"

"I don't know."

"Let's get on to another subject," Chanequa said, "let's get an apartment together."

"Where?"

"Not far from our school."

"I don't want to live that deep in the hood."

"How about midtown?"

"I'll live in midtown. What made you decide on getting an apartment?"

"My parents won't let me eat what I want. I'm trying to get on a diet."

"Why? You're not fat."

"But my ass is. When guys look at me they look at my ass. Some men think more is always better but I don't. When we went to the mall yesterday, two guys were following me. Talking about how big my booty is. I'm tired of that."

"Do whatever makes you feel comfortable about yourself. Just don't try to lose weight by starving yourself."

"No I'm not going to do that. After school tomorrow, we look for an apartment."

"I'm with that," Shonda said. After Shonda finished talking to Chanequa, RJ came by. They sat on the couch and RJ started talking. "I know last night didn't look right but I didn't sleep with her. Pete talked me into going to the club did you say Pete?" Shonda asked. "Yes."

"I don't know why you hang with Pete and the rest of them. Pete hates to see us together. He's jealous. You never knew this…Pete tried to get with me not long before we started dating. "You and I have something special," he said, "I won't allow others to break us up... so will you forgive me?"

"Yes I forgive you but this still doesn't explain what that woman was doing in your bedroom."

"I got drunk, she was willing to drive me home."

"Who is this woman?"

"My ex-girlfriend from college."

Shonda was quiet for a moment to think. "I think it's best for us to be apart for a moment."

"Why?"

"I need to think."

"Shonda, I want to be with you, just you."

Shonda got up. "See yourself out," she said before she walked away.

THE SECOND Chapter
1992

Chanequa woke up in the middle of the night. She has been seeing that Sir Mix-A-Lot video on MTV "Baby's Got Back" millions of time, it's giving her nightmares. She didn't lose the weight she wanted in the past year so Chanequa tried to make it her new year's resolution. It's 1992 now and it hasn't been going her way so far. She and Shonda had their apartment for four months. Having their own place was the only accomplishment for the start of the year. Chanequa had her waitress job at Steak n' Shake and Shonda worked at Vinone's clothing store in Crown Center. Shonda and RJ spoke every now and then. She told him every time she saw him that she still needed her space. Spring break came, Shonda was going on a trip with a guy named Cornelis she met downtown. "You shouldn't go nowhere with a guy you barely know," Chanequa said to her. Shonda does know that Cornelis was the drinking and partying type. She didn't care. She wanted to step on the wild side since she's been the good girl all her life. "Shonda please do not go nowhere with this guy."

"Chanequa get off my back. I'm tired of just going to school and working five days of the week, not doing anything else."

"The only thing you should be worrying about is finishing school."

"Look you're not my mother and I'm not in high school."

"Shonda you know nothing about this guy and you know some of these guys out here are up to no good."

"You're just saying all this because you don't have nobody and you're fat!" Chanequa became red hot and then slapped Shonda. Shonda put her hand over the spot she hit her. Shonda stared at Chanequa in shock. "I can't believe you hit me!" Shonda was about to cry. Shonda pushed Chanequa and she flew back on the couch. Shonda ran to her room and buried her face in the pillow.

Chanequa followed her and touched her lightly on the shoulder. Shonda jumped. "Shonda what has gotten into you? You should be trying to talk things out with RJ."

Shonda was just sitting there hugging her pillow. "RJ is a good man. You told me yourself before. He's human like everyone else. You can't expect him to never mess up... not that he did. We shouldn't be fighting we're friends we're more like family now."

Shonda looked at her with watery eyes. Chanequa just gave her a friendly smile. Shonda decided not to go out of town with Cornelis. She and Cornelis went to a party on a Friday night. Chanequa was at home watching Video Soul. She was enjoying it until they played Wrecks-N-Effect video "The Rumpshaker."

She hurried up and changed the channel. RJ, Pete, Sean, and Montrell went to a strip club downtown for RJ's birthday. They had their drinks and got hypnotized by all the beautifully nude women shaking all they got. One of the women came to their table. "Check her out," Sean said. A really young woman wearing a short see-through blue baby doll gown. "Anyone like a lap dance?" she asked. She happened to look at RJ. RJ looked at her, surprised. "Jayla," he said. She took off. He stood up trying to see where she where she went. "You know her?" Pete asked. RJ sat back down. "That's Jayla Simms, my girlfriend from high school. Right after graduation she dumped me for a pro football player."

RJ got up and spoke to one of the bouncers to see her. He found her for him. She had gotten dressed and was about to leave. RJ walked with her outside. "You here to chew me out?" Jayla asked. "No I didn't know you worked here. I thought you would have been living like a big star by now."

"Nope all I have now is a little boy to take care of."

"Where are you staying now, with your family?"

"My family don't want anything to do with me."

"Do you have paper and pen?" he asked. She handed a piece of paper and a pen to him from her purse. "Here's my address and phone number Call me or come by whenever you need someone to talk to."

Jayla looked at the paper he gave her. "Thanks you're a good man RJ."

He saw to it that she got into her little car and she drove away Shonda was not feeling comfortable at the house party Cornelis brought her to. He and everyone there were drunk and she was so scared. Shonda stood away in a corner to try to stay invisible. Cornelis came stumbling over to her. "I'm leaving," Shonda said. "We haven't been here that long," he said. "We've been here long enough. I need a phone to call a cab."

"You don't need to call a cab, I'll take you home."

"You're drunk."

"Come on there's a room, I'll sleep it off back there."

"What am I supposed to do?"

"Just stay with me. You don't have to be around all these people."

They went to the room. Cornelis sat his drink on the on the night stand and then shut the door behind them. Shonda sat on the bed. Cornelis laid on top of her started kissing her. "Cornelis stop. Stop! Get off of me!"

"Girl you know you want some of this."

She clawed him. He got off of her. Shonda ran out of the room, out of the house Cornelis ran after her. "Shonda wait! I didn't mean it. I brought you here I'll take you home."

"Leave me alone Cornelis you're still drunk."

"I haven't had that much to drink. Besides, you don't live far and it's a little dangerous to be out here by yourself."

Cornelis started driving her home. Everything was going alright at first, then he started swerving while going down Swope Parkway. He had cut a car off and then the car hit them from behind. They ended up running into a pole and Shonda got a bump on her head from hitting the window. Shonda opened her door. Cornelis had a hold of the tail end of the jacket she had on. She broke free from him. Shonda ran across the street to a payphone in front of a liquor store. She stayed there until her cab showed up. Cornelis took off before the police arrived Chanequa was fast asleep on the couch with the TV still on when Shonda got home. Shonda went to her room, sat on her bed and began balling. Chanequa had woken up, heading for the bathroom. She saw Shonda's bedroom light was on. Shonda tried to act like she wasn't crying when Chanequa walked in, by looking down at the floor. "Back so soon?"

"Yes."

Chanequa knew something was wrong by the way she answered. "Shonda is everything okay?" She started crying out loud," No!"

"Did he do something to you?"

"He tried to take advantage of me and I got into a car accident."

"A car accident!"

"I have a bump on my head that hurts like hell."

"Where is he?"

"I don't know. I caught a cab home from Swope Parkway where we had the accident."

"How did it happen?"

"I think he was drunk."

"You had to know he was drunk. Must you be so naïve."

"I wish RJ was here," Shonda said, "I miss him."

Chanequa calls RJ from the phone in the kitchen. "Hi RJ It's Chanequa. I know it's kind of late, could you please come by, it's urgent."

RJ came as soon as possible. "Thanks for coming." Chanequa hugs RJ. "Shonda misses you. Nothing has been going right for her since you two have stopped speaking."

"Where is she?" RJ asked. He followed Chanequa. She peeked her head through Shonda's bedroom door. "RJ is here to see you."

"RJ! You called him over here didn't you? I can't face him right now."

RJ walked in. Shonda turned her head. He sat next to her on the bed. "You want to talk?" he asked. Shonda just turned to him and laid her head on his shoulder. "I didn't mean to be that way."

"I know, I know," RJ said Shortly after RJ and Shonda got back together, RJ paid Pete a visit. He never got a chance to get with him about his little set up with Ginger. "Hey RJ what brings you by on this joyous day?"

"Pete, Pete, Pete…you are something else Pete. Why did you want me to meet Ginger at the club?"

"Pete, I need to go to the store," Pashay said, interrupting them. "Not now," Pete said. Pashay folds her arms. "It was no need for that especially when you tried to talk to Shonda before I started dating her."

"You tried to talk to who?" Pashay asked. "Nobody," Pete answered. "and I never done that."

"Well I choose to be with Shonda so don't mess with me or her again!"

"Pete, I need to go to the store!"

"Leave me the fuck alone!" Pashay stomped out of the living room. Early Saturday evening, RJ had nothing on except a towel wrapped around his waist, talking on his cordless phone to Shonda from her job. "What time you're getting off?"

"In thirty minutes."

"I might be still in the shower by the time you get here so I'll have the door unlocked."

"Okay I'll be there soon."

After RJ got off the phone, he put on his robe and house slippers. He took the trash out then went to the backyard to feed Manni. She quickly devoured her food. "You're a feisty girl aren't you?" RJ went back in the house, picked up his cordless phone, and ordered some Chinese. Then he finally got in the shower. Five minutes into his shower, RJ thinks he's hearing footsteps. He doesn't pay it any attention so he continued soaping himself. Then the footsteps were heard again. "Shonda!" He heard nothing but the water running. RJ stood still waiting to hear the footsteps again. "Is that you Shonda?" The footsteps continued towards the bathroom.

RJ pulled back the shower curtain and a woman was in his bathroom.

"Jayla what are you doing here?"

"I'm sorry for barging in on you like this but I saw that the door was unlocked."

"Yeah maybe I shouldn't have left it unlocked anybody can walk in on me. "I hoped you didn't mind because you said I could see you whenever I needed someone to talk to. "Yeah but it would have been nice if you called first."

Jayla was staring at his equipment. RJ put his hand in front of it and then hid behind the shower curtain. Then he poked his head from behind the shower curtain. "Do you mind waiting out in the living room?" Jayla came closer to him. "Come on RJ I want to stay." She was hugging him then she was feeling on his ass. "I use to love watching you on the football field in those tight pants and how we use to do it in bed."

"Well that's the past. Now I'm expecting my girl I'm expecting company so I'll see you sometime."

"I'm not company?"

"You're an unexpected guest."

RJ grabs his towel and wraps it around his waist. He tries to show her the way out of his house. When they were going through the living room, Jayla pulls him down on top of her on the couch. She was kissing the mess out of him. RJ was trying to get up, but she held on to him tight. Then his towel had come off. He made her let go. "RJ I don't want to leave."

RJ gets up and Shonda just walked in. She sees them two on the couch, gives RJ a mean look and storms out the door. "Shonda no! Don't leave!" He wanted to go after her but couldn't. She was already gone. "Does this mean I can stay now?" Jayla asked RJ went to the Blackwood's the next day. "Mr. Blackwood, I have a serious problem...I think I'm cursed."

"Cursed," Redmond said. "Yeah this been the second time Shonda and I broke up because of my exes. She thinks I'm sleeping with them because I've been caught both times in bed with them though I haven't done nothing with them. Ginger and Jayla are both aggressive women. They don't take no for an answer. Shonda's not like neither one of them and I love her but I've lost her."

"You haven't lost her. You just have to show her that she's the only woman for you."

"I don't know what I can do."

"You'll think of something. You're a smart man RJ. Be sure to let those know that it's not their decision to interfere in your life anytime they want. A good woman is hard to find just like a good man is hard to find. Take it from someone who's been married for 33 years. There's only one kind of love and that's real love."

For many days, Shonda haven't been active nor social. Every night she'll be in tears. One night she couldn't sleep at all because she wouldn't stop crying. Chanequa sat with her. RJ has been having a tough time figuring out how to win Shonda's affection back. He knows he has to come with it because what she saw happening on his couch was just unexplainable. RJ showed up on her job but they said she was on vacation for a week. He talked to Chanequa on the phone. She told him Shonda went to Tulsa and she'll be back on Sunday. RJ just got an idea. "What time on Sunday?"

"Three, three-thirty," Chanequa said. "I've got a special surprise for her."

Shonda caught the metro back home from the bus station, late Sunday afternoon. Chanequa was gone. The apartment smelled like scented candles. Shonda sat her little suitcase on the living room floor. Then she headed towards her room and opened the door.

She was shocked at what she was seeing. Her room was decorated erotic like, like a love scene in a movie. The twelve scented candles that made the place smell so good and lit up the place. The rose petals scattered all over the bed and R Kelly's song "Honey Love," playing on the radio which set the mood just right. Shonda turned on the on light and blew out all the candles. It was romantic but didn't want the place to burn down. A present was sitting on her dresser with an envelope laying on top of it. She knew this was the work of RJ. The envelope read "I'm sorry." In the inside was a cute card that read "something to make you feel special love RJ. Shonda opened the present. She pulled out a sensuous nightgown. Shonda loved it. What some guys would do to win your affection. The year has been flying by. Chanequa hasn't been sticking to her diet. Milkshakes and fatty foods been calling her name. She didn't really gain any weight anyway. Chanequa didn't care anymore. She realized she'll always have a big butt no matter what. The only good thing for her before summer ended she got a better job down in the Plaza at Tomfooleries. Once fall rolled in she was really rolling in some money. Then Chanequa had fallen for a customer named Jamod on a Friday night. She found someone that appreciated her for her service not for her bottom. They went out twice out of the week. Everything was going good so far, except Jamod's pager would go off all the time but he would ignore it. Chanequa brought Jamod to RJ's New Year's Eve party at his house that he and Shonda put together. Everyone else got there before them. Chanequa and Jamod didn't arrive until after ten. Everyone was sitting around in the living room, listening to music, with food spread across the table for everybody to dig into and the TV on Dick Clark's New Year Eve's Times Square. Chanequa had introduced Jamod to everyone when they first got there. Everyone was laughing and enjoying themselves. By eleven fifteen everyone had quieted down. Montrell and Sean were cuddled up with their women. Pete and Pashay started smacking each other and calling each other names. RJ and Shonda were all lovey dubby with their champagne glasses in their hands. Jamod was watching Chanequa eat some Gates ribs. "You're really getting down on those ribs."

"Excuse me?" Chanequa asked. "Why don't you take a moment from those ribs and let's get close." Jamod put his arm around her.

Chanequa wiped her hands on a paper towel, then Jamod's pager went off. He ignored it. Jamod started sniffing her neck. "You have on some nice perfume." Jamod's pager went off again. He looked at Chanequa.

"Could I use your phone?" he asked.

"Yeah, in the kitchen," RJ said.

Jamod went to the kitchen and made his phone call.

Chanequa was curious to who he was talking to because he was in the kitchen for a long time so she got up. Pete was staring at Chanequa as she walked pass. Pashay smacked him in the head. "What you do that for?" Pete squealed. "You better stop looking at her ass!"

"Will you two cut it out," RJ said. Chanequa stood in the doorway of the kitchen. Jamod had his back to her still on the phone saying "I know, I know I'll be there as soon as I can."

He hung up after that. Jamod was startled when he saw Chanequa standing there with no expression on her face. "Who was you talking to?"

"One of my kids have gotten sick. I have to go." Jamod went back to the living room. "Sorry everyone I have to leave…emergency. Happy New Year's."

"Happy New Year's!" Everyone said.

"Be careful out there," RJ said.

Chanequa stood there looking at the door after Jamod went out Everyone was wondering why Chanequa was just standing there looking at the door. "Chanequa aren't you going to sit down?" Shonda asked. Chanequa slowly walked over to sit at the end of the couch all by herself. "Cheer up baby girl it's almost a new year," Sean said. "I wonder what 1993 is going to be like," Montrell said. "We're about to find out," RJ said," in five, four, three, two, one...

THE THIRD Chapter
1993

Chanequa was trying to spend time with Jamod but he was always like," something's come up."

"I promise on Valentine's Day we're going to spend the whole day together," Jamod told her. Valentine's Day came. Not one phone call or anything. RJ and Shonda had gone out. Pete and Pashay cooked at home and rented movies to watch with the kids. Sean and Montrell got laid. Just another upsetting Valentine's Day for Chanequa The day after, Chanequa was home alone, reading an Essence magazine. Jamod then decided to show up. "Chanequa I'm sorry we didn't get to spend Valentine's Day together."

"What happened?" she asked. "Something came up."

"Something always come up with you. You that busy."

Someone knocked on the door. "Who could this be?" Chanequa asked herself. She peeked through her peek hole. A woman was there. "Who are you?"

"I'm looking for Jamod," the woman answered. "Who is this woman?"

"My babies mama..... can I answer the door?"

"What is she doing here?" Jamod didn't answer. Chanequa opened the door. "Jamod can you hurry up. Me and the kids are ready to get home... it's cold out here." She walked away. "You have the nerve to show up here with your babies mama but couldn't spend time with me on Valentine's Day. I'm sure that's who you were with."

"Chanequa listen-- "Get out Jamod."

"You don't understand."

"Get out Jamod! Lucky for you I'm a Christian because it could of gotten real ugly up in here."

Jamod exited out the door. Late spring, Chanequa and Shonda had finished their two years at Penn Valley. Chanequa had a degree in Sociology and Shonda in Art Design. By summer, Shonda moved in with RJ. Chanequa felt kind of lonely without her there but she needed her own space. Lately Pete has been coming by RJ's complaining about Pashay. It was on a Sunday when Pete had an ice pack held against the back of his head. "I have had it with that female!" Pete said to RJ. "What happened this time?" RJ asked. "Me, Pashay, and the kids were at Hypermart today in the produce section. This woman walks pass and Pashay thought I was looking at her chest because she had big boobs and was attractive. So she hit me in the back of the head with an orange."

RJ started laughing. "This isn't funny. I've got an headache that won't go away."

"You two behave like kids and you should be apart because you guys can never get alone."

"You can say that again. If I stay with her any longer, I'll have life in prison for murdering her ass."

"You'll be alright," RJ said Chanequa and Shonda spent their summer shopping. They even went on an all girl trip to Dallas with Shonda's Aunt Tee, her twin cousins Relisha, and Kelisha for the Fourth of July. RJ flew to Atlanta to visit his parents. By the end of the summer, RJ, Shonda, Chanequa, Sean, and Montrell went to Oceans of Fun and they had a ball. As the holidays drew near, everyone was making plans. "Would you like to fly to Atlanta for Christmas?" RJ asked Shonda while they were at home watching TV. "Atlanta yeah," she answered. "I've told my parents so much about you. So they're really anxious to meet you."

"I wait to meet them too, but what about Thanksgiving? I can't cook."

"That's no problem. Mrs. Blackwood invited us and Chanequa certainly wants us to come."

"Great I can't wait," Shonda said. Thanksgiving came. RJ and Shonda went to the Blackwood's about 2 o' clock after watching some of the Macy's Thanksgiving parade on TV. They pigged out then left after two hours. Then they headed to Shonda's Aunt Tee's house. Her house was full of relatives Shonda hasn't seen in years. They didn't eat or stay. RJ and Shonda went to the Plaza for the lighting ceremony but it was too cold outside for Shonda and way too crowded so they went to the movies and after that called it the night. The day after, Shonda worked a ten hour shift. She sat down on a bench in front of the store, rubbing her feet. One of her co-workers, Patsy was leaving out. "I am not ready for anymore of these long hours we have to work," Patsy said, "I'll be glad when Christmas is over."

"Same here."

"Well I'll see you tomorrow," Patsy said. "See you tomorrow."

Once Shonda walked into her place, she couldn't wait to soak her feet in some warm water. The house was dim. RJ was asleep on the couch, laying on his back hugging the newspaper. Shonda lightly touched his face. RJ flinched then woke up. "Hey I was wondering when you were coming home. I was getting bored too death without you here."

"Well I'm here and my feet hurt—bad."

"Don't worry I'll run you some warm bath water and massage your feet."

"I'd like that."

For the whole month, Shonda did nothing but work her little feet off. She was in need of foot massages everyday but she enjoyed seeing everyone out spending their money on their loved ones. Speaking of loved ones, Shonda made sure she got RJ a nice gift, a silk robe and some silk boxers to go along with it.

She wondered what he was getting her. Christmas was five days away and they were spending four days in Atlanta which was really going to be the time of their lives. December 21st. RJ and Shonda just boarded their flight to Atlanta and it was almost time for take off. "I am so glad we're doing this…spending all this time in Atlanta on Christmas and meeting your parents."

"I also booked us a us a three night stay at the Holiday Inn," RJ said. "We're not staying at your parents?"

"Oh nooo… it's going to be too many people there anyway. Christmas time is the time spend with your family but there is never a wrong time to make some love." RJ had a horny look on his face. Shonda started smiling. "You're going to get something started on this plane."

"Sorry we have to wait," he said. Atlanta was a little colder than Kansas City It started snowing a little not too long after they got there. They checked into their hotel, then RJ called over to his parents for them to come get them. RJ introduced them to Shonda when they arrived. "This is Shonda Lloyd my girlfriend."

"It's so nice to finally meet you. RJ says so many great things about you," his mother Jaleece said. "My baby is such a nice boy." His mother pinched his cheek.

"Mama please."

"RJ is our only child but for this Christmas we're going to have a house full of relatives."

"Well let's get to the house before everyone else shows up," his father, Dean said. Nobody showed up except for a cousin of RJ's. She, her husband, and their two kids then decided to stay at their hotel until Christmas Eve. RJ's parents gave Shonda a tour of their home and then they all went to three different malls which took up their whole day. RJ and Shonda was brought back to their hotel. RJ took a shower, then Shonda took one after him. While she was showering,

RJ got comfortable in the bed with his boxers on. "There's some clubs we can go to tomorrow night. My cousin Theresa will take us."

"Great," she from the bathroom. Forty-five minutes passed by. Shonda was still in the bathroom. RJ dozed off then he came out of his sleeping spell. "Shonda are you still in the bathroom?"

"Yes."

"What's taking so long?"

"I'm not ready yet."

"Well I'm horny so hurry up."

RJ turns on the TV. He goes through some of the channels then turns it back off. He lays back, getting impatient. Shonda finally comes out in a turquoise silk robe that touches the floor. Then she starts twirling around over to his side of the bed. "You like?" She has her hands on her hips. "Yeah but I don't know why you got prettied up for because we're about to have some mad sex."

"I want this night to be special and plus I want to talk about something."

"Can you talk your way out of that robe?" RJ tries to untie her robe. Shonda pulls away and walks to her side of the bed. "Damn it! What is it you want to talk about?" he asked. "You know I've been on birth control…but now I'm on my very last pill."

"So you're getting some more, right?"

"I wasn't planning on to because I want us to have a baby, RJ."

"A who?"

"A baby."

"Shonda this isn't the right time. We're on vacation. Let's have some fun. A baby is something we can have in the future. Right now we have some business to take care."

"You want to have sex without an rubber but you don't want to have a baby."

"Shonda why are you making this so damn complicated?"

"I'm not doing anything, goodnight." She turns off the lamp."

"So it's like that. Fine forget you." RJ rolls over.

Shonda runs to the bathroom, shuts the door sits on the floor, and begins to cry the next night, Theresa and Darren took RJ and Shonda to a club. It was so crowded it was barely room to dance. RJ and Darren took turns dancing with Theresa. Shonda didn't want to dance. She was still upset with RJ. She sat by herself at their table drinking a rum with Coca-Cola. RJ sat across from her drinking some of his drink. "You want to dance?" he asked. "No," Shonda answered. "Let's not be like this. We've hardly talked all day," RJ said. Shonda wasn't listening. She was gazing at everyone. RJ didn't say anything else. He just leaned back in his chair. Shonda saw what he was leaning back for. He was checking out some woman on the dance floor. The woman kept smiling back at him. Shonda grabbed her purse and went to the restroom. She stares at herself in the mirror. Then she puts on some lip gloss trying not to think about what's going on the last two nights in the hotel, they didn't have sex. What made Shonda more upset with RJ was he didn't want them to spend two more days in the hotel. He'd rather stay at his parents for Christmas Eve and Christmas. December 24th RJ's parents house was crowded with people. Aunts, uncles, and cousins of his were decorating the place. Shonda appreciated being around his family but RJ paid her no attention since they've been at his parents house. Later everyone gathered in the living room with the fireplace going, sitting around watching classic Christmas movies. RJ and Theresa were throwing mints and peanuts at each other. Shonda played patty cake with Theresa's kids. When it got late, everyone went to sleep. Shonda couldn't sleep for nothing. She was trying to get to the bathroom without stepping on anyone.

Shonda was going pass the kitchen. RJ was sitting at the kitchen table drinking some wine. "Shonda."

Shonda went into the kitchen. "Why you still up?" She asked. "I'm not tired," RJ answered. "I knew you couldn't sleep because you kept tossing and turning."

Shonda stared at him. "Sit down."

She sits in a chair next to him. "RJ are you mad at me?"

"No why would I be."

"I thought you were mad because of of what I said at the hotel."

"Naw we'll have children when the time is right."

RJ had his hand on the table. Shonda reached out and rubbed it. She loved how soft it felt and it was sexy how his veins popped out. "Come here," he said. Shonda sat on his lap. They started kissing. RJ didn't want to stop but Shonda had to. "There's an empty bedroom upstairs," RJ said. "We should wait until we get back to Kansas City."

"Shonda I'm drunk and I want some right now."

"What if I get pregnant? I'm not on the pill anymore and I know you didn't bring any condoms. Let's just go to sleep…it's almost Christmas."

"You go ahead... I want to finish my wine December 25th. Everyone opened presents and exchanged presents. RJ opened his present Shonda bought him. "Damn this is nice. I like this."

"I knew you would," she said. RJ kissed her on cheek. Shonda then was waiting for her present. "I'm sorry I tried to get you a present. Everything was so picked over, I couldn't get you anything."

"It's okay, it's the thought that counts, right," Shonda said with disappointment. "Girl I'm just playing with you. I just wanted to see your reaction... merry Christmas." RJ handed her, her present.

She pulled out two piece string bikini. "I love it but I can't wear it anytime soon."

"Of course you are. It's for places...I bought us some roundtrip tickets to Miami in February for Valentine's Day."

"Really RJ?"

"Yeah the tickets are at home."

"I love you," she said. "I love you too. Now the second place is for that private party we've talked about. Me watching you behind the video camera with that two piece on in your heels on. There are so many good things to come for the both of us."

Shortly after everyone opened their gifts, the table was set and the food was ready. Everyone took their seats but wasn't allowed to touch anything yet. RJ's parents were the only ones standing. "Okay I want everyone's attention," Jaleece said," Dean and I are grateful for having you all here to celebrate Christmas and we hope we get to celebrate more Christmases like this."

"Let's say grace," Dean said Everyone held hands and bowed their heads. After grace, Dean carved the turkey. Everyone had a feast. They all decided to the movies except RJ and Shonda because they was ready to head back to Kansas City. Jaleece and Dean hated to see them leave. RJ and Shonda slept through the plane ride. Their place seemed different to them when they got back. Those four days being away from home, was going to make everything seem different for now on.

THE FOURTH Chapter
1994

RJ's house was packed for his Fourth of July swimming pool party with some R Kelly music playing. RJ was cooking on the grill, Shonda and Chanequa brought out a cooler of Budweisers. Sean and Montrell were in the pool playing beach ball with a lot of women. Pete and Pashay were sitting at the picnic table not speaking to each other. Chanequa went back into the house and sat alone on the living room couch. She just couldn't enjoy herself like everyone else because she had to keep a towel wrapped around her waist to hide the few extra pounds she gained in the last four months. Chanequa had nothing but depression for the past year of having no man and feeling unattractive. She was beginning to envy RJ and Shonda's relationship because of what they have. She really wished she have gotten with RJ instead. How could I have allowed Shonda to have him? I've known RJ before she did. Then Shonda came in the house. "Chanequa what's wrong?"

"I'm just not in the partying mood."

"Well please get in that mood. I'm not going to let you sit here."

"I want to be alone."

"Well did you eat?"

"No I'm trying to lose weight."

"Why are you trying to lose weight? You're not fat."

"I feel fat."

"You should eat something. Starving yourself is not good."

"I'm not starving myself, I'm just not hungry… can we not talk about this? I just want to be left alone."

Shonda heads back outside just when some commotion started. RJ was standing in between Pashay and Pete because they were about to fight. "If you two are not going to chill out, it's best you leave."

Shonda took Pashay inside. RJ stared at Pete. "What is up with you two? You need to keep your business at home.... you're messing up my party."

Pete walked away. He was about to get into his car that was out front then RJ called his name. Pete was going to ignore him and drive off but didn't. "Is there something going on at home?" Pete was looking elsewhere. "Come on Pete I'm your boy, you can talk to me."

"I lost my job two weeks ago. Pashay just found out two days ago. She's threatening to kick me out, keep my kids from me… all I ever tried to do was do right by her, be a family man. What did I do wrong?"

"I know you haven't done nothing wrong. Have you tried to find another job?"

"Yeah. I've got a couple of interviews."

"I'll help you out with some more jobs this week coming up but right now I want you to come back and have some fun. Shonda is talking to Pashay so everything should be alright." RJ pats him on the back as they went back to the party. Pete circled some jobs in the newspaper while Pashay was playing with the kids in the living room. Chanequa steps out the shower at her place onto the scale. Still dissatisfied with her weight, she heads for the kitchen and eats a donut. Shonda was lying in bed, pulls back the covers, lifts up her nightgown, and starts pulling off her panties. "Not tonight Robert."

"Robert! Who the hell is Robert?"

"Sorry I meant to say RJ. You've been listening to too much R Kelly. You still on birth control? "Yes and why?"

"I was thinking we try making that baby we've talked about."

"Why now?"

"I think it's time we have a little one running around here."

"We should get married first," Shonda said. "So now you want to get married?"

"That's the way it's supposed to go."

RJ rolled over. "What is it with you RJ?"

"First you want a baby, now marriage. That's too much right now."

"What's the difference we live together."

RJ walked out of the room Three months have passed. Chanequa forced herself to stick on a diet. She even exercised every day. A month ago, Chanequa met a young Caucasion guy named Bradley in Prairie Village who became just her sex partner One early Saturday morning about two-thirty they came from a club to Chanequa's place to have sex. A hour later they just laid in bed, exhausted. Bradley started smoking a cigarette. "You want one?" he asked, offering her a cigarette. "No thank you I don't smoke."

Chanequa wants to ask Bradley a question but is frightened. She looks over at him. He's looking so relaxed, puffing on his cigarette. "Do you think I'm pretty?"

"Yeah you look alight."

Alright wasn't the answer she was looking for. Alright to Chanequa was like not telling the truth. It was her big bootie that he's interested in. She was at the point in her life where she didn't care anymore. Chanequa liked having someone to lay with every weekend. Then she would feel bad. Her mother didn't raise her to be some man's sex toy. Chanequa never did like after every time they had sex, Bradley smoked or got drunk, rolled over and went to sleep. Shonda and Chanequa met at Chanequa's job on a late Monday afternoon.

Shonda wasn't saying much. "So, what's been going on with you lately?" Chanequa asked. "Nothing much but work. What about you?"

"I'm making it. Is something on your mind?" RJ has been acting different for a while because I want to get married and have a baby."

"I'm sure he wants the same. He's just not ready."

We've been together damn near six years. Now we're just living together. If now isn't the time, when is?"

"You're asking the wrong person. I haven't been in a relationship in so long, I don't remember what it's like. But you shouldn't worry. You'll have that big wedding and some children soon. Be patient."

"Chanequa you're such a good friend and a good person. I've been praying God sends you the right man."

Chanequa smiled. "I know he will."

Chanequa stopped over to Shonda's and RJ's place with a grocery bag full of candy for the trick-or-treaters. Shonda had all the horror movies picked out for them to watch. RJ was sitting on the couch looking crazy. "I hate Halloween," he said.

"Well I like Halloween," Shonda said. "I love seeing the children in their cute little costumes."

"Wake me up when Pete gets here. I'll be in the room taking a nap."

RJ leaves the living room. "You're right RJ is acting different," Chanequa said. "I'm worried about us."

"Don't worry about anything."

"I mean we've been trying to make a baby and nothing has happened. I've had irregular periods in my late teens…something's wrong. "You think you can't have children?"

"Yeah."

"You should go get looked at before you can say you can't have kids."

The doorbell rang. Shonda answered the door. "What's up? Happy Halloween," Pete said. "Happy Halloween Pete come on in."

Pete gazed at Chanequa as soon as he walked in. "How are you Chanequa?"

"I'm good."

"You look nice," Shonda said to Pete. "I'll get RJ for you."

"So Miss Chanequa…. You got a boyfriend yet?"

"I don't want to talk about that."

"Look at you, looking all sharp," RJ said just entering the room. "Life's been good to me."

Pete slapped a twenty dollar bill in RJ's hand. "I owe you that."

"You don't have to give me this."

"Yes, I do. That's why I came over here. I have to get going. My kids want to go trick-or-treating at the mall." Pete turned to Chanequa. "Maybe we can talk sometime."

Chanequa gave him I don't think so look. He left. "Can we talk right quick?" Shonda asked RJ. "Shonda I'm tired right now."

RJ goes back to bed. Shonda and Chanequa get comfortable for the horror movies for the night Shonda was watching RJ pack up his suitcase. "Why at the last minute you're deciding to spend Christmas and New Year's in Atlanta?"

"Because…"

"Because what?"

"I'm just going alright."

"I thought you were spending the holidays with me."

"Christmas is about spending time with your family. If you wasn't such a selfish girl you would know that."

"Why are you talking to me like that? What have I done?" RJ closed his suitcase. He went to the living room, put on his coat and took out his keys. Shonda was right behind him. "Will you talk to me?"

"While I'm gone you should try figuring out what you have to do to give me a baby. I have a plane to catch."

Shonda was confused Shonda spent Christmas with her Aunt and twin cousins. Tee tried to talk Shonda into going down to Tulsa to see her parents. Shonda never had a good relationship with her parents. Although she does want to try to have one. Now wasn't the time. All she could do was think about RJ. After being at her Aunt's house all day, she went home, feeling lonely. The next minute, RJ called. "Merry Christmas," he said. "RJ! What a surprise."

"You miss me?" he asked. She hesitated. "Yes."

"I want to say I'm sorry for the way I've acted."

"It's okay. You coming home soon?"

"I'll be back New Year's Day. My mother is having these get togethers so I got to stick around."

"What's that noise?" Shonda asked. "What noise?" RJ asked. "It sounds like a woman is moaning."

"Oh that's nothing."

RJ turns the porno he was watching, off. "Well I gotta go babe, love you."

RJ hangs up quick. Shonda stared at the receiver then hung up. RJ was in bed in a hotel with a woman lying next to him, running her fingers through his hair. Then she started kissing his neck. "Why did you have to have the TV up? You knew that was my girl on the phone."

"So she can hear the fun we're having," she said. "Don't do that again," RJ said. Tee, Shonda, and Chanequa met up with Pete, Montrell, Sean at the Marriot on New Year's Eve. Pete was feeding his face. Montrell and Sean were showing off the women that they were with. Chanequa stayed seated to herself. She kept her jacket on because she thought she was showing too much and was feeling uncomfortable. Shonda and Tee came to the table with a plateful full of food. "Are you going to eat?" Tee asked. "No I'm going to take a cab home. I'm starting to feel sick."

"Don't spend your money on no cab," Shonda said. "I don't want you to have to leave the party."

Shonda called Pete over. "Pete was you about to leave?" Shonda asked. "Yeah here in a minute."

"Chanequa needs a way home."

"No thank you I'm taking the cab."

"Why the cab? I'll take you home."

"As long as you take me straight home."

"Of course… ready when you are."

"Take care of yourself," Shonda said giving Chanequa a hug. Chanequa tried to remain silent during the ride. Pete kept looking over at her. "You doing okay over there?" he asked. "No," she answered. "What's wrong?"

"I'm not feeling well. I'll go in and get some money for you," she said when they got to her place. "That's alright. I don't need anything. What's really going on in your world Chanequa?" You not really sick are you?"

"Why you think that?"

"You don't look sick."

"How do you know how I feel? I just want to be alone tonight and get some rest."

"I know you don't want to be alone on a New Year's Eve, do you?"

"No, not really."

"How about I keep you company?"

"Fine."

They went up to her apartment. Chanequa turned on the lights and the TV. "You like something to drink? I have some champagne."

"Yes I do. I knew you weren't sick girl. You're trying to set the mood?" Pete flopped down on the couch Chanequa had two tall glasses and the bottle of champagne. She sat the glasses on the table. "Let me," Pete said when she was about to open the champagne. He poured the champagne and then they held up their glasses. "Here's to a new beginning," Pete said. "A beginning of what?" Chanequa asked.

"Of us being good friends. I've always liked you Chanequa. I want to get comfortable." Pete took off his coat.

"You going to take off your jacket?" She stands up and takes off her jacket. "You look good. You look like you've lost some weight."

"Yeah I've finally got down to the size I wanted. But now I don't feel good about it."

"You're a beautiful woman. I don't understand why you're never happy with yourself. You may think I'm just looking at your back side like these other guys but I've always only saw you."

58 "That's nice Pete but I know you're in a relationship."

"Me and Pashay have been through for months. I got a good job, my own place and I only speak to Pashay when I want to see my kids."

"I see. You don't expect me to believe you?"

"No I guess not but how I feel about you is no lie."

"Oh look at the time! It's almost midnight and I've haven't made my New Year's resolution yet," Chanequa said. "I've made mine…. Be my girl."

Chanequa played like she didn't hear him. She was drinking up her champagne. It was finally struck twelve. They heard gunshots and fireworks go off. "Happy New Year's," Pete said. "Happy New Year's," Chanequa said. He poured some more champagne in their glasses. Pete was drinking slow, Chanequa was drinking way too fast. He took her glass from her, then sat the glasses on the table. Pete kissed her. Chanequa couldn't believe he did that. Then she thought it's a New Year so what the hell. They kissed so passionately, then they ripped each other's clothes off.

THE FIFTH Chapter
1995

Chanequa was woken by the doorbell. She hated to move. She was laid up in bed with her head against Pete's chest. Pete was still asleep. She put on her robe and headed to the living room. Chanequa peeked through the window. She opened the door. "Chanequa honey are you okay?" Shonda asked, hugging her. "I've been worried about you."

"I'm fine. I was just very exhausted."

"It doesn't look like you've got much sleep."

They heard footsteps and a door shut. "Is somebody here with you?" Shonda asked. "Ahh sorta, kinda," Chanequa answered. Then they heard the toilet flush and the door opened. Pete comes in the living room with only pants on. "I thought I heard another voice," Pete said. Shonda started smiling and giggling. "I can't believe it…you two…together?" Pete put his arm around Chanequa. "She's my sunshine." Then he kissed her on the cheek.

"I'm so happy for you two. Well I'm going to run along. I didn't mean to barge in on your romance. Have a nice day," Shonda said with an even bigger smile on her face when she left. "Now she's going to tell everybod y," Chanequa said. "This is going to be a good year," Pete said. Super Bowl Sunday was happening at Pete's. Montrell, Pete and some cousins of theirs were sitting around waiting for the game to start Sean was talking on the phone. RJ hasn't shown up yet. Chanequa and Shonda had came in. Chanequa had two cases of Bud Light. Shonda had a bag of groceries. They sat the stuff on the kitchen counter. Pete came into the kitchen going through the grocery bag asking "Whatcha got, whatcha got?"

"Just some junk food," Chanequa said. "You got the beer though."

Pete took one of the Bud Lights out of the case. Chanequa was into eating her candy bar when he put the beer bottle against the back of her neck. Chanequa jumped. "Boy stop!" Chanequa and Pete were both laughing. Then they both started kissing and hugging. Shonda was like, "Okay I'm leaving Chanequa…catch you later."

"Alright girl," Chanequa said. They continued hugging and smooching. Next the doorbell rang. "Shonda probably forgot something," Chanequa said. "Maybe it's RJ," Pete said. Pete answered the door. Pashay and the kids were at the door. "How come you don't stop by to see your kids anymore?" Pashay asked. "Pashay now is not the time."

Pashay saw Chanequa. "Oh I see you're into something else."

"Pashay you need to leave. We're about to watch the game."

"I'll leave but I'll be back later."

"You ain't coming back here."

"Oh yes I am. You need to spend time with your family."

"You need to give the horse back it's hair."

All the guys were laughing."

"You go to hell with your smart comments."

"You're probably be there before I do."

Pashay rolled her eyes at him and Chanequa, then she left. Pete got comfortable for the game. Chanequa went to the bedroom and shut the door. RJ was laid back on the couch watching TV. Shonda sat next to him. "What are we going to do this Valentine's Day?"

"I don't think it's a good idea for you to sit close to me. I think I'm coming down with the flu."

"You need me to get you anything?"

"No I'm alright."

That night Shonda slept on the couch because RJ locked himself in the bedroom. For the first time she and RJ were distant. They haven't been love making in months. The next day, Shonda cooked a pork chop dinner when they both got home from work. "I got something from Hardee's."

"What's wrong RJ? You don't want to eat my cooking, you don't want to touch me…Is there somebody else?"

"Of course not."

"Then what's the problem then?"

"You haven't given me a baby yet and I'm tired of waiting."

"What do expect me to do?" We haven't had sex in months anyway."

The phone rings. RJ answers it. It wasn't good news because RJ had an upsetting look on his face He hung up the phone and said, "I got to go to Atlanta…my father is sick."

RJ flew to Atlanta two days later. It's been quiet and lonely around the house for Shonda. It seemed everyone was sick with the flu. Shonda stayed tuned to the weather channel on the major inches of snow that they were about to get. She went grocery shopping and she packed the refrigerator with food and drink. Shonda phoned RJ to see if he was going to make it back before the snow hits. "No I just found out that my father has prostate cancer."

Shonda was silent then she said, "I'm sorry to hear that."

"My parents and I just got back from the hospital. I'm going to stick around just for another day."

"See you when you get back."

"Take care," RJ said. It was a very cold weekend. RJ was laid back on the couch being very quiet with the TV on low volume. Shonda comes up behind him with her arms around him. "We can do something to take your mind off everything," she said. RJ said, "No." He got up and walked away.

RJ remained the same when spring arrived. The romance had really went away. RJ just came inside the house from cleaning the garage when Shonda and Chanequa came from the City Market with a bunch of bags of fruits and vegetables. RJ was drying his hands with a towel because he just got through washing his hands wondering why they were bringing a lot of bags in the kitchen. "Hi RJ," Chanequa said when she walked passed him. RJ didn't answer back. "What's all this?" he asked. "Fruits and vegetables. A lot of stuff we can make with them," Shonda said. "Shonda I don't know why you bought all this stuff because you can't really cook anyway."

"How dare you!" Shonda threw a tomato at him. She was about to throw something else at him but Chanequa stopped her. "No worries. I wasn't going to throw anything else…I was going to stick this squash up his ass. You've been nothing but a jerk towards me for many months and I've had it."

"Come walk with me outside," Chanequa said. They went outside. RJ stared down at the smashed tomato on the floor. "That doesn't seem like RJ in there," Chanequa said.

"For the past seven months he's been so cruel to me. Guess he's still upset about wanting to have a baby. It's not going to happen."

"Why you say that?"

"Because I can't have children."

"Are you sure?"

"Yes. I haven't told him I told him I couldn't have children yet. Right now he's dealing with the fact that his father has cancer."

'Oh my," Chanequa said. "What next?" Shonda asked. "Things will get better… just wait and see." Chanequa said At the moment things didn't get better. By mid- June, Dean Richardson lost his battle to cancer. Jaleece chose to have his body flown back to Kansas City where he was known most. His funeral was at a funeral home on a pretty Saturday afternoon. Family members and others headed over to RJ's house afterwards. Redmond, Sidney, Eugene, and Chanequa shared their sympathy. Pete, Montrell, and Sean just stuffed themselves with all the good food that was there. After everyone went home, Shonda helped Jaleece, Theresa and some other family members of theirs clean up. RJ was sitting in the living room looking at all the sympathy cards when Shonda came to see how he was doing. Shonda sat next to him. They stared at each other for moment She touched his hand. Then she hugged him saying, "I'm here for you baby."

RJ didn't say anything. Being held was what he needed. RJ used his week vacation from his job to help drive his mother back to Atlanta. He flew back to Kansas City before his vacation was over. He had some news for Shonda. "I'm moving to Atlanta. I found a job but I haven't gotten a place yet. I want to be near my mother since my father isn't around anymore."

"So that's it… you're just going to leave. What about us? Is it over? I knew it… I knew you were tired of me."

"Shonda listen…I don't want you to come with me to Atlanta unless…unless you'll be my wife." He had a little box with a ring in it.

"Are you for real?" Shonda asked.

"Yes."

Shonda kept gazing at the ring. "You going to marry me or what?"

"Yes I will."

They hugged. "But I have to tell you something…I can't have children."

"That's okay, we got love…love for life."

Shonda and RJ began making wedding plans immediately. RJ's plan at first was to go downtown and get married but when they announced their engagement to everyone they knew, Eugene insisted on marrying them at his church. It was a simple inexpensive wedding with all their family members and friends. That evening Pete and Chanequa drove them to the airport so RJ and Shonda could head off to their honeymoon in Las Vegas. This was going to be Shonda's first time in Las Vegas. Being married just made it more exciting. When they checked in their hotel room, Shonda dropped her luggage and flopped back on the bed. "I can't believe we're here in Vegas."

"Well believe it sweetheart," RJ said. "What should we do first? Maybe we should check out the action and attractions that's happening," Shonda said. "Wait a minute, wait a minute, this is our wedding night. We can sight-see tomorrow. The only action happening is in this room," he said. They started to get close. "You know what happens in Vegas stays in Vegas," he said. "Yeah I know."

"I don't want you to think about anything except us, alright."

"Alright."

He gave her a kiss. Back in Kansas City, Pete and Chanequa were in bed sleep, when someone came knocking on the door. Pete woke up to answer the door. "Pashay what are you doing here? It's one o' clock in the morning."

"I need to talk to you."

"Why don't you just pick up the phone?"

"You hang up in my face every time I call."

"Because you want to act foolish every time we talk."

"Well I want us to work something out."

"What? Why?"

"I want you, me, and the kids to be a family again."

"It's a little too late for that, don't you think."

"It's that big booty bitch isn't it? I know she's in there."

Chanequa was standing in the bedroom doorway listening to what was being said. She heard the front door slam. Chanequa quickly got back into bed. Pete climbed back into bed not saying anything. "Who was that?" Chanequa asked. "Nobody just go to sleep."

"I can't sleep right now."

"Why?"

"I just can't."

Pete sighed. "Are you alright?" Chanequa asked. "I'm good."

"Pete can you hold me?" He embraced her as she tries to go back to sleep. The newlyweds got relaxed in the bathtub. RJ was washing Shonda's back. "That feels so good," she said ," let's go to sleep in the bathtub."

"I don't think we should," RJ said. "Why not? This is so comfortable."

"We haven't made love yet."

"We can do it in here…standing up in the shower."

"Baby I'm not trying to slip and fall in the shower."

"It's a lot of different positions I want to try. I thought we were in Vegas," Shonda said. "How many times we've done it in the shower?" RJ asked. "Lots of times, but in Vegas I thought anything can happen?"

"I'll tell you what…. we can start off making love in the shower, then on the table, then in the bed until we can't take it no more. Sounds good?"

"Yes it sounds good to me."

After the honeymoon was over, RJ and Shonda went to Atlanta so she could get settled with a new job and RJ could find them an apartment. A month later, they were ready for Atlanta. The moving process was a lot of work but they had help from friends. Chanequa was shedding tears when they were about to hit the road. "I'll call you ever week, every chance I get," Shonda said.

Shonda cried too when they hugged. RJ hugged Pete and Chanequa. After all the good-byes, RJ and Shonda finally left Kansas City.

THE SIXTH Chapter
1996

It took them a week to get their apartment arranged the way they wanted it. Shonda loved it because the apartment was more spacious than what she thought. RJ had to let his Rottweiler Manni, stay with his mother because of their no pet policy. Shonda sold her Toyota Corolla so she could get a new car here in Atlanta Married life was going good but Shonda felt lonely at times by not being able to talk Chanequa whenever she wanted. She was the only real friend she's had in her life. Shonda didn't know anyone in Atlanta. Other than working, she was stuck in the house. The club scene was out because RJ said he didn't move here to be partying. He wanted her to be a wife that worked and took care of home. Which was what Shonda did exactly, cooked, and kept the house clean. RJ got home so late every night he didn't eat when he got there. He would say he already eaten. Shonda really believes he doesn't like her cooking. Shonda got a chance to talk to Chanequa one evening. "So how are you liking Atlanta?"

"It's okay…I guess."

"You guess. You don't sound excited. That's not a good sign living in Atlanta."

"I haven't done anything exciting since I've been here. RJ wants to keep me in the house."

"What is he tripping off of?" Chanequa asked. "How are the malls? I know you've done some shopping."

"Yes I've been to the malls, no to spending money because I don't go anywhere anyway so what's the point. I just window shop."

"That doesn't sound good Shonda. I hope things change for you."

"I hope so too."

Four months passed. It's the same thing five days a week. RJ comes home about eight in the evening, takes a shower, changes clothes and watches TV. He only eats a sandwich or maybe some fruit. Shonda got curious one night and asked," You must really hate my cooking don't you?"

"I eat out that's why I'm never hungry when I get here."

"Fine I won't cook anymore except for myself."

By the time spring arrived, spring had really sprung. Shonda had just gotten home from work on a Friday. Just when she was about to unwind and get ready for the weekend, someone was at the front door. Shonda had no idea who it could be. She looked through the peephole. It looked like a woman. Shonda opened the door. She and the woman stared at each other. The woman was holding an infant. "May I help you?" Shonda asked. "Are you Shonda Richardson?"

"Who wants to know?"

"You don't know me but your husband knows me…RJ is the father of my child."

Shonda's mouth opened. "Is this some kind of a joke?"

"No this is no joke. Me and RJ had a relationship for three and a half years. I got pregnant a year ago with Richie. He's three months now."

Richie, that's what RJ's mother calls him sometimes, Shonda said to herself. Shonda started to feel nauseated so she ran to the bathroom and threw up. After that, she sat on the bathroom floor, crying RJ came home late as usual. Shonda was washing dishes. "Hey Shonda."

Shonda wouldn't look his way or talk. "How was your day?" She focused on the dishes. He knew something was up. It was the first night without the hello kiss. RJ didn't worry about it no further. He just headed for the shower RJ was getting ready to leave on a rainy Saturday afternoon. Shonda was laid out on the couch looking at a hairstyle magazine. "You going somewhere?"

"Yeah I got to go by Theresa's because she wants me to return something to my mother. I'll be back soon."

Soon as RJ left out the door, Shonda got her keys and followed him to wherever he was going. To Theresa's house. *What kind of lie is that? I know damn well if Theresa wanted to give something to Jaleece, she would have done it herself.* It was a ten minute drive to this little house he stopped at. Shonda parked behind a parked car so she wouldn't be seen. Shonda just sat back and watched. He went to the front door of the house. The lady with the baby came out. She was carrying the baby in a car seat. RJ kissed the baby on the forehead before he get them both situated in his car. After RJ got in the car, him and the lady started kissing. Shonda turned her head in hurt. Then they drove away. Shonda drove back home. Shonda has been watching the clock. It's been over six hours since RJ's been gone She's been roaming around the house, drinking and crying. She's so ready to leave. It was going to be hard. She had a lot of material things that she worked hard for and didn't want to leave behind. Shonda feels she's stuck in this big city with no one to turn to RJ decides to show up about eleven forty-five. Shonda was asleep at the kitchen table. RJ rubs her on the back. "You doing alright?" Shonda doesn't say anything. "You really need to get in bed it's late."

Shonda was really in the mood to ask him some questions but she was too tired.

Maybe tomorrow Shonda called Chanequa the next evening. "I'm so happy to hear from you," Chanequa said. Shonda was quiet. "Shonda are you alright?"

"Oh, yeah. How is everything in KC? You and Pete doing alright?"

"We're great. You and RJ doing good?"

"Ahh we're doing okay."

"Uh oh, what's wrong? Is he beating you?"

"Nothing's wrong Chanequa."

"Then why are you sounding like that?" Shonda swallows hard and then proceeds. "RJ has a baby mama that lives here in Atlanta. A baby boy that's only three months."

"Really. How did you find this out?"

"She came by here."

"What if this girl is making this up?"

"She's not. I followed RJ for proof and I seen the proof. I think this is the reason why he wanted to move here…to be close to her. I don't know what he expects me to do? Go along with it."

"What are you going to do?"

"I know I'm going to leave. I got to get my job back in Kansas City and find a place to live."

"Don't worry about a place to live. You got family here and a friend that loves you. You're room is always available whenever you need it."

"Thank you. God is good to me. I never had fear of being alone."

"Continue to keep God in your corner and he'll see you through," Chanequa said Shonda tried her best to stay with a positive mind but it was sometimes hard. She kept what she knew from RJ long enough. Shonda was lying down on the couch with her silk robe she put on after she got through with her bath. RJ comes home, and starts rubbing on her leg. "Don't touch me," she said, freeing herself from him. "Why you're my wife ain't you?"

"Why don't you go touch that woman you had that baby with. Oh yeah you didn't think I'll ever know about that?"

"I was going to tell you."

"You was really going to tell me that? We haven't been married long and now you want to show me what a dog you can be."

"I'm not trying to hurt you Shonda. You wouldn't give me a baby and she didn't want to get married."

"You are a selfish, selfish idiot!" she yelled. "You're saying if she wanted to get married you wouldn't have married me? You would have left me for her?" RJ was speechless. "What about love for life? I remember somebody saying that. I guess that was just talk. If I didn't have self-control, I would get a pot and bust you in the head. Now I'm going to get my beauty sleep. You do whatever." Shonda slammed the bedroom door.

RJ was frightened when Shonda stormed out the door on a Saturday evening. She ended up at a bar. Shonda couldn't believe she didn't realize this at first. The mother of his child was that lady in a club when they came to Atlanta three years ago for the holidays. She knew that face looked familiar. She stared down in her glass. All Shonda could see was that woman's face in her drink. A young good looking guy walked up to the bar and ordered a drink. He sat next to her and drank some of his drink. Then he looked over at her. Shonda was still staring down at her drink. He got curious. "You alright miss?" Shonda was still in her daze but a few seconds later, she then realized he said something to her. When Shonda looked at him, she suddenly started balling. They were so close to one another, Shonda found herself crying on his shoulder. He didn't know what to say. He just patted her on the back. She lifted her head when she was all cried out. Shonda cleaned her face up with a napkin. "Are you going to be alright?"

"I think so."

Shonda saw that she drenched up his shirt. "I'm so sorry I didn't mean to be crying on you." She was wiping his shirt with another napkin.

"It's okay. It's not that big of a deal. But I got to ask, what's a pretty married woman doing alone in a bar?"

"My husband is the reason why I'm here. I have serious martial problems that's forcing me to get a divorce. I haven't even lived here in Atlanta or been married barely seven months and everything has went downhill."

"Well you're just like me. I haven't even lived in Atlanta barely a year and I think the women here are so in your face types. I knew when I saw you you couldn't have been from here. You were minding your own business. I almost thought you were about to fall asleep."

Shonda smiled. "You smile? You look a lot better like that."

"Thank you. I think I'd better head home. "I appreciate this little conversation we had. It may not have changed nothing in my life but it's great to talk to someone."

"Where you from?" he asked. "Kansas City. That's where all my family, my best friend and all my love is."

"Me I'm from Mississippi. I only moved here for a change. I'm not really into the partying scene, but I have some cousins here that are party animals."

"Atlanta certainly isn't the scene for me," Shonda said. Shonda got her keys out of her purse. "Could I walk you to your car?" If you want to."

He walked her to her car. She got in and rolled her window down. "Quentin Kenson is my name. I never introduced myself."

"Shonda Richardson."

They shook hands. "Listen, I come here often through the week. If you ever want to conversate about anything, this is where I'll be."

"Okay," Shonda said. "Have a safe drive home," Quentin said. "You too."

Shonda drove home When Shonda returned home, RJ had a confused look on his face. "What's the deal with you?" he asked. "Nothing hun…I just needed to get out. I've been cooped up in this house long enough. I'm better now."

RJ followed her to the bedroom. Shonda sat on the bed, undressing. RJ stood there with his arms folded, watching her. "So talk to me where you been?"

"I just went to a bar… what else you want to know?" Shonda stood up to slip on her nightgown. Then she went to the bathroom to brush her teeth. He followed her there. "I want to know do you still love me?" She spit the toothpaste in the sink with the water running and answered, "I've been wanting to ask you the same thing."

RJ walked away. Shonda didn't have no idea what he was thinking Shonda didn't go back to the restaurant bar where she met Quentin at. It's been two weeks since she's been. Shonda didn't feel it would be right meeting a guy anywhere and still being married. It was Thanksgiving time. They went over to RJ's mother's house. Theresa, Darren, and their children came. Shonda and Theresa worked together on preparing the food in the kitchen. Darren and RJ were watching football in the living room. Jaleece sat at the kitchen table cleaning chitlings while Theresa's kids were tasting what was left of the cake mix out of the mixing bowl. Everything was ready by one thirty. The table was set and everyone was seated. The door bell rang. RJ got up to get it. Shonda was sitting the potato salad on the table when RJ let in little miss thang and his baby Richie. Everyone was staring at the lady and baby. Shonda was shocked and mad. "Mom do we have room for another person?" RJ asked. "Ah sure," Jaleece answered. RJ wouldn't look at Shonda. "I'll put the baby in the bedroom so he can finish his nap," Jaleece said. "I have to run to the store before it closes I forgot something," Shonda said. She grabs her coat and rushes out the door. Shonda wait a minute," RJ said. Shonda was long gone An hour and a half later, Shonda haven't returned. Jaleece was cleaning the table while RJ's baby mama, Shia was finishing her sweet potato pie. Theresa kept gawking at her, then pulled RJ to the side. "Why you let her come here?"

"I wanted her to bring Richie."

"You couldn't have brought the baby on your own?"

"Shia won't let me take the baby nowhere without her."

"But your wife… "my wife wasn't going to come at first."

"RJ you're my cousin and I love you but you disgust me."

Theresa and her kids went to the living room where Darren was. RJ turned to Jaleece. "Mama can you take me home?"

"What's wrong?"

"I need to find Shonda."

Jaleece looked over at Shia. "What are you doing about her?"

"She can drive her own self home."

"Take some food home to your wife… you hear me?"

"Yes ma'am."

Shonda was sitting at the kitchen table with her arms folded and with a half empty bottle of wine in front of her when RJ got home. "What happened to you?" RJ asked. She turned away from him. "She only came to bring the baby."

Shonda didn't say anything. "I brought you some food."

Shonda grabbed her wine and called it a night. Two days before Christmas, Pete, Chanequa, Sean, and Montrell were at the KCI airport waiting for Shonda to arrive. "What time is she suppose to get here?" Pete asked. "Two fifteen," Chanequa answered. "We've been here for forty minutes," Sean said. "It's only two thirty-five," Chanequa said. "You guys looking for me." Shonda was standing behind them. "Shonda!" Chanequa hugged her. "When did you get here? We was getting worried."

"I caught an earlier flight and I've been looking around in the gift shops."

"We're glad you made it," Chanequa said. "I'm glad to be back in KC."

"What's RJ doing?" Montrell asked. "He's been into a lot things. He's very busy."

"Mama, daddy, and Eugene will be happy to see you. You and I also have some things to talk about," Chanequa said. "I can't wait to tell you," Shonda said. Shonda went back to Atlanta the day after Christmas. RJ wasn't at home so she went to the bar where she met Quentin. Shonda went three nights straight, but never seen him. Shonda was relaxed on the couch, watching a movie on a weeknight when RJ sat next to her. "I never got to ask you how was your Christmas in Kansas City?"

"It was great. I got to see everybody and everyone asked about you."

"Really. My Christmas was great too. We had a house full of people. I wish you could have been there. "Oh so you can surprise me again."

"She didn't come this time."

"Probably because you knew I wasn't going to be there."

"Let's not fight about this."

"Why not? You had the nerve to flaunt that floozie in my face." Shonda got up and threw a pillow at him. "I want a divorce," she said. "You want a who?"

"A divorce. I'm not happy."

"You don't want to do that," RJ said. "Yes I do. You're playing double-dutch with me and her and it's not fair."

"I don't want you to leave me."

"It's too bad. That's how I feel now."

The next evening, Shonda was getting out of the shower. RJ starts taking pictures of her. "What are you doing?" Shonda asked. "I'm taking pictures of my beautiful wife. I love it when you're soaking wet."

"Can you please not do that?"

"What do I have to do Shonda?"

"There's nothing you can do. You had a baby. That's unforgivable. So if you don't mind I'd like to finish drying off."

She shut the bathroom door in his face. This time Chanequa flew to Atlanta so she and Shonda could go out for New Year's Eve. They got there to the club very early to beat the crowd. Chanequa drank a lot and danced with different guys. Shonda enjoyed just being out for the very first time. Ending the year out with a bang and was going to be midnight in the next ten seconds

THE SEVENTH Chapter
1997

It's 1997. When the balloons dropped, everyone really started partying. Chanequa and Shonda stayed for thirty more minutes then left. Shonda ran into Quentin outside of the club. "I've been missing you," Quentin said. I'm sorry I've been not wanting to come out. Quentin this is my friend Chanequa from Kansas City."

"Hello," Quentin said. Chanequa said hello back. "It seems this year is going to be good because I'm seeing you," he said. "Can you meet me at our spot tomorrow?"

"If you'll be there, I'll be there," Shonda said. "Most definitely. Happy New Year's."

"Happy New Year's," she said. "Is that your something on the side?" Chanequa asked, after Quentin left. "No he's not."

"He's such a handsome stud. Don't worry I won't tell RJ."

"He's just a friend."

"I wish I could be just like you…a husband and a friend."

"Cut it out Chanequa."

"Don't be ashamed Shonda, it's a brand new year."

They got back to Shonda's place before 1 a.m. "That was a whole lot of fun. I got something to talk about when I get back to KC," Chanequa said. RJ was standing there waiting up. "I want to talk to you," he said. "I don't want to talk."

"Please Shonda."

"Maybe I should get me a room," Chanequa said. "No I'm not letting you stay in a hotel," Shonda said, "it's your last night here anyway. I'll make up the couch for you."

"Thank you I appreciate this."

RJ folded his arms Shonda met up with Quentin the next evening. "I hope you like barbecue?" Quentin asked. "Of course. I grew up in a city that has nothing but the best barbecue."

Quentin drinks his beer as she eats some of the barbecue. "How is your New Year going so far?" he asked. "Good."

"Have you got to really see Atlanta?" he asked. "No." "How about I show you?"

"When?"

"Right now. That's if you can."

Shonda thought about it for a second. "No. I don't know you well enough."

"You think I want to do something to you? I'm not trying to, but I understand. Maybe some other time perhaps."

"I really like you Quentin but I'm about to get a divorce and I'm trying to decide if I want to move back to Kansas City or get a place here."

"Whatever your first mind says, but for me I'd like you to stay."

Shonda loved the smile he had on his face. Shonda was about to leave work and gotten some flowers sent to her that said "Happy Valentine's Day," from who she didn't have no idea. She certainly didn't think it's from RJ. They've been so distant. Shonda left the flowers in her car when she got home. RJ was there, which surprised her. "How was work today?" RJ asked. "It was alright."

RJ had a box of chocolates and a bouquet of roses behind his back. "Happy Valentine's Day," he said when he showed them to her. She took the candy and roses. "Thanks."

"I made reservations," he said. "Reservations for what?"

"I'm taking you out. We need to spend more time together. We need to restore our marriage."

"Sorry I don't want to."

"Why do you keep being so tough with me?"

"Hello! You did have a kid with another woman."

"How many times are we going to go through this?"

"How would you like it if I had a baby by another man?"

"You can't even have kids."

"You know what I'm getting at. Forget it!" Shonda drops the roses and chocolates on the floor Shonda got a phone call at her job from Quentin. "You like the flowers I sent you?"

"Yes I love them but you didn't have to. How did you know where I worked?"

"I seen you there before. I wanted to say hello but you were busy. You like Italian food?" Quentin asked. "Yes."

"I can cook some good lasagna. You want to come by this Saturday and try some?"

"I'd love to."

"Come about seven."

"I'm there."

Shonda showed up at Quentin's place at seven on the dot. She stared at the door, too frightened to knock. She stood there for about five minutes when Quentin opened the door. "Hey you're here," Quentin said. "Yes I was just about to knock."

"Come on in. He lead her by the hand to the kitchen. He had the table set up with two lit candles. Quentin pulled out a chair. "Sit."

"This is nice," Shonda said when she sat down. "Do you always do your ladies like this?"

"Yes because romance is my middle name. Now this is still pretty hot so be careful."

He dished out the lasagna. Shonda tried to take a bite of the lasagna but put it back down. "It is too hot. I'll wait until it cools off a little bit."

Quentin sits. He eats some of his lasagna. "So do you know how to cook?"

"I think so. My so called husband doesn't think so. He doesn't seem to think too highly of me. "Oh yeah then why did you get married?"

"I did love him. "We've been together for nine years, married over a year now. I found out something after we moved here. Which is the reason why he wanted to move here and the reason I'm going to divorce him."

Quentin fed her a piece of lasagna off of her plate. "Is it alright?"

"Yes good and not too hot now. So what part of Mississippi you from?"

"Biloxi. I loved it there."

He ate up his lasagna. Shonda was halfway through hers. "Do you mind if I take some of this home with me?"

"You ready to leave already?"

"Doesn't it bother you that I'm married?"

"Not if it bothers you. Are you afraid he's going to find out about me?"

"No. it's just a little too soon."

"I'll get you something to drink before you leave."

Quentin got some cranberry juice out of the refrigerator then poured it into the plastic cups sitting on the table. "I have been a little too forward. Maybe I should back off. I hope things work out for you but if you really decide to leave him, I'll be here."

Shonda felt his hand on her thigh. It was like he was massaging it because his hand was strong. It almost made her want to stay but she had to go. In the month of March, Shonda got her money together and flew to Kansas City to file for her divorce. When she got back to Atlanta, she began looking for an apartment in the apartment guide. Then she asked Quentin to take her to check out the places. Shonda had just gotten up on a late Saturday morning. RJ was in the living room putting clothes in some suitcases. "What are you doing?" Shonda asked. "I'm leaving. I seen the papers.
You want to divorce me, go right ahead. I can't live under the same roof with you."

"I told you I was getting a divorce…you thought I was joking?"

"It don't matter. I'm outta here."

Shonda called Chanequa. "RJ left."

"For good?" Chanequa asked. "I don't think so. I think he's doing this for two reasons…one he's doesn't think I can afford to keep this place by myself so he's just trying to punish me. He wants to see me come crying to him for help."

"I don't know what makes him think you can't survive on your own. He's forgotten what an educated black woman you are."

"We both are," Shonda said. "Yeah we're some hard- working women that make a lot of money."

"Amen. That man better recognize who he's messing with," Shonda said. "He'll get it sooner or later," Chanequa said. "Let's talk about the other guy."

"What guy?"

"You know what guy, the cute guy with the cute ass that I seen on New Year's Eve."

"Oh that guy," Shonda got quiet."

"You slept with him have you?"

"No Chanequa I haven't. The only thing I'm thinking about is getting through this divorce."

Shonda went to Quentin's place. "You hear from anyone yet?" Quentin asked. "No…my husband moved out."

"Oh is that a good thing or a bad thing?"

"I don't know. He seen the divorce papers."

"What are you going to do?"

"Stay there at the apartment, see this divorce through. That's all I want. I'm going back home…I just came by to tell you this."

"No Shonda, stay."

"Quentin even though my husband is out doing wrong, I don't feel I should commit adultery."

"How is this adultery? You want him out of your life and the way I feel about you is certainly not a sin."

"I want to know more about you," Shonda said. "I'm just a guy that grew up in Mississippi. I had an abusive childhood. My daddy was a mean man. He would try to hit my mother. So I would take the beatings for her. I wasn't going to stand back and watch no man hit her. I would never hurt you Shonda."

"What about the other women?"

"Other women, what do you mean?"

"You must have other women."

I had other women, not anymore. I know you probably don't believe me because of what you're going through. I like uniqueness. None of those women I use to date weren't. Your husband probably has more than me but that doesn't matter. I couldn't stab you in the back like that. I'm not trying to tell you to forget about your husband and come go with me but I want to love you the right way, the way a man is supposed to love a woman." He laid a soft kiss on her. "Now I want you to think about this before you go to bed tonight."

Shonda showers before she decides to go to bed. She thinks she hears the phone ring so she tries to hurry out of the shower. Shonda accidently slips and bruises her shoulder. She doesn't pay the pain no mind. Anxious Shonda stood over the phone shivering naked, waiting for a ring. She looked at the caller ID. No one even called. When Shonda finally went to bed, she couldn't go to sleep. She could hear the front open. Then RJ clicked on the bedroom light. "What are you still doing here?" RJ asked. Shonda sits up. "What do you mean? I live here."

"Why do you want to live in my house and then try to divorce me?"

"This is my house too. You walked out."

"I'm going back to be with my family." He said.

Shonda rolled her eyes when he left. Shonda went over to Quentin's when she got off work. "You smell so good," he said, hugging her. Quentin wanted to kiss her on the neck so he pulled back her shoulder strap and saw the bruise. "What's this?" he asked. Shonda pulled her strap back up and said, "it's nothing but a bruise."
"Yeah but how did you get it?"

"I fell in the shower."

"Don't give me that I fell in the shower stuff."

"I did fall."

"Your husband hit you, did he?"

"No honestly, he didn't."

"The real reason I wanted you over here today was to ask you something."

"Like what?"

"I know it's kind of soon…but I was wondering if you wanted to come to Jackson, Mississippi with me in July?"

"What for?"

"My family reunion."

"I don't know I have to go to Kansas City on the twelfth of that month."

"We'll be back way before then because it's on the fourth."

"Will they like me?"

"I don't see why they wouldn't. Besides you wanted to know more about me. You can see where I come from."

"But in the meantime, what do we do?" Shonda asked. "You tell me," Quentin said Shonda found an apartment and temporarily worked a part-time job to buy things to decorate her apartment. Four months later, Shonda was packing up for the trip to Jackson. At first she and Quentin have been dating for a minute, Shonda got comfortable with it. They took a bus there, checked into a motel and then headed to the family reunion. It was a lot of people and lots of food. Quentin introduced Shonda to his mother, his brother, and a lot of other relatives. By evening the DJ showed up to start up the party after everyone got their bellies full. He played a little bit of old school rap, some R&B such as Aaliyah, and Adina Howard. Then he slowed it down with some Marvin Gaye. "Is your father still around?" Shonda asked as they were dancing. "No he died three years ago. I don't miss him. Let's get out of here. I don't want to use all my energy dancing," Quentin said. They went to their motel to make love. "You have any energy left?" she asked after they finished. Quentin started laughing. "Why you want to go another round?"

"No I'm satisfied. Let's go to sleep. We have a long day ahead of us."

Shonda and RJ finally went to court. RJ had his lawyer, Shonda just had Chanequa there supporting her. The divorce proceedings didn't take long because she didn't want or need anything from him. Shonda was so relieved when she and Chanequa was standing out in front of the court house. RJ walked past her, giving her a look. "I'm not getting married again, at least not for a long time."

"I'm glad you're not with him anymore and I have some great news…Pete and I are having a baby."

"Wow, really," Shonda said. "Yes I'm two months now."

Shonda hugged Chanequa. "This is some great news."

A week later, Shonda had just got home from work. RJ shows up. "What's been up with you?" RJ asked. "You miss me already?" Shonda asked. "I just wanted to know what really made you want me out of your life? I've been watching you Shonda. I've been knowing about your little boyfriend and the recent honeymoon you two been on."

"Get out of my house!"

"Listen!" he shouted. "I don't want to listen to you, get out!" RJ quickly leaves. She knew that wasn't the end of it. RJ hasn't come around her for a moment but she has this big feeling he's still watching her. Three weeks from the time he shown up at her place, he showed up at her job. Shonda didn't see him at first because he was watching her from a distance. When she was heading out for her lunch break, she seen him and tried to avoid him. RJ followed her. Shonda tried to act like she didn't know he was following her. He called her name. She looked back. "I told you to stop bothering me."

"I know you like it when I chase you."

"No I don't. I can get you for harassment."

"Why it got to go there? We're known each other too long."

"I don't want you anymore RJ so go away before I go there with you."

"Alright you will regret this."

He left Shonda and Quentin kissed each other goodnight before she left his place on a Friday night. "Sleep tight," Quentin said. "You too," Shonda said. Shonda got into her car, started it up. Before she could drive away, RJ jumped into the car. "It's not safe to leave your doors unlocked. Anybody can jump in the car with you and hold you hostage."

"Where did you come from?" Shonda asked. RJ put his arm around her. Shonda was looking around. "Don't worry your boyfriend ain't looking."

"What do you want from me?"

"Just your time." He was feeling on her thigh and then moved his hand under her skirt. "Remember when I use to finger you?"

"Stop touching me!" She moved his hand. "Why?" He touched her again. Shonda clawed him on the side of his face. "What the hell you do that for?"

"Go before I call the police!"

"You're making things worse," RJ said. He got out of the car, rubbing his face. Shonda couldn't see where he disappeared to. All she wanted to do was hurry home and lock herself in. For the last couple of days, Shonda has been paranoid. She was at her dining room table, eating and every little noise she heard made her heart pound. The knock on the door almost made her spill the plate of pork chops and collard greens. Quentin stopped by. "Baby what's wrong? You look like you're scared. "My ex-husband has been harassing me and following me everywhere I go even to your place."

"Is that so. Where is he staying?"

"Where we use to live. I hope you're not thinking about going over there?"

"I'm just going to talk."

"But still," Shonda said. "Has he been making any threats?"

"No,"

"Okay show me where he lives."

Quentin goes to RJ's place. RJ stares at him like Quentin just disturbed him. "What do you want?"

"I want you to leave Shonda alone."

"Why?"

"Because I'm telling you."

"Like I'm really going to stop because you say so."

"You're the one asking for it" Quentin said. RJ starts laughing. "Get away from here youngster." RJ shuts the door on him.

Quentin went back to Shonda's. "What happened?" she asked. "Nothing. I just told him to leave you alone but he didn't take me seriously."

"I know that isn't going to solve anything," Shonda said. "As long as he's not threatening you, you have nothing to worry about."

She puts her arms around him. "As long as I have you near me, I know I have nothing to worry about."

They kissed Shonda was surprised RJ hasn't been bothering her for a while but it always occurred to her that he still could try again anytime. She stayed in town for the holidays and spunt it with Quentin's people. New Year's Eve it was just them two at her place. Shonda wanted a quiet and private year ending celebration with all the champagne she could drink.

THE EIGHTH Chapter
1998

Shonda was glad that there was no bad weather during her flight to Kansas City. She had to see her best friend's brand new baby girl. Shonda and Chanequa gazed at her smile. "What's her name?"

"Chanelle."

"Cute," Shonda said. "Pete calls her his little Valentine."

"She has Pete's nose," Shonda said. "She looks like her daddy, period. Pete just left before you got here. I tell you Shonda, when I gave birth to Chanelle, Pete took her in his arms and he was filled with so much joy."

Shonda saw the tears in Chanequa's eyes and it made her cry too. When Shonda left the hospital, she was kind of envious because of her not being able to bare children. What a curse Shonda returned to Kansas City by summer and brought Quentin with her. She introduced him to Pete, Sidney, Redmond, and Eugene. Pete and Chanequa took them to the Bannister Mall and the Ward Parkway Mall. Shonda and Quentin were going up on the escalator and three teenage girls were in front of them looking back at Quentin. He pulled Shonda close to him. "You want to help me pick out some shoes?" Quentin asked. "Yeah," Shonda answered. He kissed her on the cheek. The girls turned around and got off. After from leaving the mall, they all went into midtown to the plaza. "How do you like Kansas City so far?" Chanequa asked. "I like it especially here in the plaza," Quentin said. "Do you like going to the zoo?" Shonda asked. "Yes but it's been a long time since I've been to a zoo," Quentin said. "That's where I want to go."

"First let's finish walking here," he said. Chanelle starts crying. Pete takes her out of her stroller. "She probably needs to be changed," Chanequa said. Pete sniffs the pamper she had on. "No she needs a nap," he said. "Let's go home it's hot out here anyway," Chanequa said. "We're going back home."

"Go ahead, we'll be fine," Shonda said. "We'll catch you two later," Pete said. "Bye," Shonda said. "Finally, we're alone. I can talk sexy talk to you," Quentin said. "Let's go back to our hotel room. It is pretty hot out here. "We're not going to the zoo?"

"No it's getting late and we're going out tonight remember."

They got their rest at the hotel. Later they went to Westport until two in the morning. Luckily, they got up in time for Sunday church service. Eugene did the sermon that day. Then after church service, they went Chanequa's parents' house for dinner. By late afternoon, Quentin and Shonda packed up and flew back to Atlanta. They stopped at Shonda's place. "I enjoyed this weekend," Quentin said. "Me too," Shonda said. He took her by the hand. "I really feel like we're getting to know each other more. I love how we connect."

They kissed. They continued to kiss for a while. Shonda wanted to stop. "As much as I want to, I can't. I have to get some rest for tomorrow."

"I understand. I need some rest too. Quentin gave her a quick kiss. "Goodnight."

"Goodnight," she said. What a man, Shonda thought to herself after he left. Shonda was going to unpack but she rather wait until tomorrow. She showered and afterwards she put on her bathrobe and turned on the TV. When she was about to get comfortable someone was knocking at the door. "Who is it?" She didn't hear an answer. She looked through the peep hole but didn't see anyone. Shonda slowly opened the door but kept the chain up. RJ was looking at her through the slightly opened door. "What are you doing here?" Shonda asked. "I need to see you."

"Okay you see me now go away."

"I want to come in and talk."

"It's too late for that."

"Just for one minute and I'll leave."

Shonda let him in. "Make it quick."

RJ was looking at her place. "How was your trip?"

"RJ what do you want?"

"Did you just get out of the shower? I always loved to see you soaking wet." He smells neck. "You always smell good too. That turns me on." RJ kisses her neck.

"RJ stop."

He kisses her on the mouth and they fall back on the couch. He unties her robe. She closes her robe. "Stop trying to fight me!" RJ yells. The anger in his voice made her tremble. He unzipped his pants and she let him do what he wanted to do to her. She was crying and was biting her bottom lip to keep from screaming. RJ got up forty minutes later. Shonda was laying there, shaking. "That wasn't so bad, was it?" he asked, zipping up his pants. "I didn't hurt you, did I?" Shonda wouldn't say nothing. "I'm going to come back this week to see you."

He kisses her on the forehead and leaves. Shonda just lays there on the couch. She didn't sleep a wink that night Shonda was out of focus at work the next day. All her co-workers could tell she wasn't herself. Every time she would have a moment to herself, she would cry. The times Quentin wanted to cuddle, she would pull away. She would sit at home hoping RJ wouldn't show up at her door. She knows not to let him in ever again. Next time she was going to call the police but he hasn't returned.

She had spoken with her Aunt Tee and Chanequa about returning to Kansas City for good. Quentin was overwhelmed when she told him that she was leaving. "How come you haven't been talking to me? Is it something I've done? Tell me."

"No it's not you and I don't want to talk about this now."

"What do you mean you don't want to talk about this now? What is it with you Shonda? I thought we were in love."

"Let's just say good-bye," Shonda said, wanting a hug. Quentin backs away. "I'm not saying good-bye." He walks away. Shonda put her notice in at her job and took all what she could with her. Shonda told Chanequa what happened soon as she got to Kansas City. Chanequa embraced her. A relationship was the last thing she was getting into. Shonda moved in her Aunt Tee and she worked two jobs. Three weeks passed and she was thinking about Quentin. She wanted to call him so bad but she was afraid of his reaction. Shonda was starting to feel miserable without him. She called him but got the answering machine. This was the year of misery but it went by like a bolt of lightening.

THE NINETH Chapter
1999

It's all about work for Shonda and the months kept going by Shonda took a trip to San Diego in the summer with her Aunt and twin cousins. By fall, Shonda stayed in the house all the time, thinking about Quentin. She thought she had lost his number but kept it written down in a notebook in her drawer. She called him. Nothing but the answering machine. At least she knew he hadn't moved nowhere. She tried calling a few more times. The same thing. *I know he got to be there sometimes. He must don't want to talk to me,* Shonda would say to herself. She gave up for the moment.

Pete and Chanequa put together a Christmas party at their place. The first to show up was a surprise visit from Pashay and Pete's two older kids. "Merry Christmas," Pashay said to Chanequa, "is Pete here?"

"Yes come in."

His kids ran to him. Pete gave them hugs. Chanelle gave them hugs too. "Hi Pete, it's been a long time."

"Yeah," he said. "Could I help with anything?" Pashay asked.

"Sure. I could use some with the turkey," Chanequa said. Chanequa and Pashay went to the kitchen. Montrell and Sean arrived with their women. Then Shonda showed up with a bag of gifts. Pete had her put them under the Christmas tree. "Chanequa's in the kitchen," he told her. "Merry Christmas," Shonda said to Chanequa and Pashay. "Merry Christmas," Chanequa said, and they hugged. "I was wondering when you were going to show up. I'm going to go out here and set up this table."

Shonda and Pashay stayed in the kitchen. "Wow Pashay you look so different now."

"I feel like a whole new person," Pashay said. "I recently got baptized."

"Really that's great."

Chanequa comes rushing back. "Guess who just walked in the door?"

"Who?" Shonda asked. "RJ."

"What?"

"I didn't know he was coming," Chanequa said. "If you don't want to stay, I'll understand. "I can take it," Shonda said. All three of them went to the living room. RJ was amazed to see Shonda again. She would hardly look at him. Everyone had Christmas dinner not long after everyone arrived. The guys had their conversation and the ladies were having their conversation. RJ over to Shonda. "Shonda, can we talk privately? I know you probably don't want to but I need for us to talk."

They went into one of the bedrooms. RJ closes the door. "Don't close the door," Shonda said. "I'm not going to do anything to you."

Shonda sat on the bed. "I'm sorry for what happened the last time we seen each other. That wasn't me and I've been drinking that day. Shila didn't want me in her life anymore and got me for child support. I took it out on you. I've took a lot of things out on you. You didn't deserve any of it." RJ got on his knees and held her hand. "I want us to be together again."

"I forgive you RJ but it will never be like in the beginning and I'm certainly not going to be your fall back. So if you excuse me, I have a party to get back to."

Shonda left the room Chanequa and Shonda flew to Atlanta the day before New Year's Eve. They got a rent-a-car so Chanequa could go shopping but Shonda wanted to see Quentin.

Shonda agreed to go shopping with her if Chanequa agreed to go by Quentin's place. The shopping took all day. It was almost nine when they got to his place. He was coming out when she just got out of the car. "Shonda," he said "Well didn't expect to see you again."

"I'm so happy to see you," Shonda said. "I've been calling you…you must be still mad."

"At first. I'm not going to stay mad forever."

"What was you getting into tonight?" Shonda asked. An Indian woman came out of his apartment asking "Are you ready to go?"

"In a minute," he said. "I'll be in the car waiting," the Indian woman said. "Guess I came at the wrong time," Shonda said. "She's just someone from work that invited me to a party."

She stared at him. "You still in Kansas City?"

"Yes. I came back because I left on bad terms. I want to do this over again. I've been missing you like crazy. There wasn't a day that went by, I could take my mind off of you."

"How long you're in Atlanta?"

"The day after tomorrow. But I don't want to say good-bye."

"Then don't. Give me something to remember."

"Like what?" He gives her a big kiss. They kissed for a long time. "How sweet," Chanequa said. "I love you," Quentin said. Shonda smiles and said "I love you for the rest of my life."

Blood Is Thick, Water Runs Thin

Late spring of 1987, Vernon Thompson parks his Lexus in the driveway of his house. He brought his younger brother Vincent, from Kansas City, Kansas back with him. "Here we are," Vernon said. "Nice house Vernon. I'm glad you're letting me stay until I can find a place."

"It's nothing, you're my brother."

Vernon helped Vincent with some of his luggage out of the trunk. "So what's your fiancée's name again?" Vincent asked. "Amber."

They sat the luggage down when they got in the house. "Amber!" Vernon called. Amber came from the bedroom. Vernon gave her a kiss on the cheek. "Amber this is my brother Vincent I told you about."

"Yes I'm so glad I'm finally meeting you," she said giving Vincent a hug. "Vernon talks a lot about you, how he can't wait to get married," Vincent said. "I'm very excited also," Amber said. "Amber why don't you show Vincent to his room."

"Sure follow me."

Vincent follows Amber. "Wow this looks nice," Vincent said when he saw the room. "I fixed it up myself," Amber said. Vincent was checking out the poster of Vanity on the wall. Then he sat on the bed. "This is comfortable," he said. "That's what I want you to feel is comfortable. Well I'm going to let you get settled in. I'm going to start dinner."

"Alright," Vincent said. Vincent unpacked then he washed up when dinner was ready. Vernon was at the table with his knife and fork eyeing the plate of meatloaf in the middle of the table, like a dog ready to grab a hold of it. The three of them got full. Amber looked at clock in the living room.

"It's getting late," she said, cleaning the dirty plates from the table. "Chesna is coming by so she and I can go to the mall."

"To the mall…this late," Vernon said. "Yes."

"For what?"

"Chesna wants to get some new Keith Sweat tape"

"Then what do you need to go for? Let her go by herself."

"I'm going because I want to go."

"Why do you always have to go wherever she goes?" Vernon asked. "Vernon, you know me and Chesna grew up together so we do everything together."

He stared at her for a moment. "Don't be gone long."

Chesna and Amber went to the mall and Chesna bought the cassette she was looking for. "Let me get back home," Amber said. "We got an hour left before the mall closes. I want to look in some clothing stores," Chesna said. "The clothing stores for what? I thought all you wanted to get was that tape."

"Yeah but I want to get something to go out in."

"Okay but hurry up I have to get back home."

"Why because of Vernon? Must you do everything he says?"

"He's my man," Amber said. Chesna tries on six different outfits by the time she made up her mind. "Ma'am the store is closing in five minutes," a sales associate said. "Alright," Chesna said. "So, who are you going out with?" Amber asked. "A lady named Lindsey from work."

"I thought it might have been a guy you were going out with since you're trying to dress to impress."

"I'm trying to catch a man."

"You going to that one club down the street?" Amber asked. "Yeah, you wanna go?"

"I can't."

"Of course you can, you're a grown woman."

"I'm not dressed."

"You look alright. All you need is a little bit of make-up."

"I'm not trying to impress nobody. I just want to have a little fun," Amber said. "Good let's go back to my place," Chesna said. Vincent was sitting on his bed, putting on his tennis shoes. Vernon knocked on his door. "Come in," Vincent said. "Hey you want to go out and get a drink?" Vernon asked. "Sure."

"I know this one spot that's not far from here. We're not going to be there long. Amber probably be back when we get back. "Yeah we can chill and talk about some things," Vincent said. "Yes I'm ready when you are," Vernon said. "I'm ready to dance," Chesna said, when they got to the club. "I see some cute guys I want to dance with," Lindsey said. Chesna and Lindsey got on the dance floor while Amber just stood back, watching. Vernon and Vincent arrives at the same place not too long after they did. The both of them sit at the bar and bought their Budlights. "So when are you starting your new job?" Vernon asked. "Tuesday. Monday is my orientation," Vincent answered. "What are you going to be doing?"

"Shipping and receiving. Same old thing I've been doing back in KCK."

"You'll love it here in Tulsa. It's nice and peaceful."

"How's everything going at the barbershop?" Vincent asked. "Good. I may have lost some customers but I've gained some new ones, still I have my regulars but other than that nothing's changed."

"That's cool," Vincent said, taking a sip of his Budlight. "Let's talk about Amber. Where did you meet her at?"

"At a church picnic two years ago."

"She's a church going girl?" Vincent asked. "Yeah Baptist. She's so sweet and smart and she does what I say, gives me what I want when I want it. That's why I can't wait until we get married so she can start having my kids. Right now she's on birth control but everything's going to change when we get married."

"Does she work?"

"At Walmart in the jewelry department. "She's going to stop working and stay home, taking care of the kids."

"How many kids you plan having?"

"Two. Boy and girl, hopefully."

"You and Amber discuss this? About having kids right after you get married?"

"No. I'm a forty year old man. I don't have time to waste."

"Do you ever see Willy?" Vincent asked. "Willy," Vernon said. "Yeah your son, my nephew."

"Every blue moon Shantal don't like me speaking to him but I got a chance to speak to him about two weeks ago. He just turned sixteen. He got himself a girlfriend. Something you should be trying to do Vincent."

While they were conversating, Amber was still sitting down, watching Chesna and Lindsey dance. "Would you like to dance?" a guy asked Amber in her ear. "No thank you," Amber answered. "Come on… I know you didn't come here to watch everyone else dance."

Michael Jackson's song, "Lady In My Life" came on when they stepped out on the dance floor. Vincent was drinking his beer when he saw Amber on the dance floor, dancing close with a guy. Vernon was still looking at Vincent, talking away. Vincent looked back at him with a scared look on his face. "What's wrong with you?" Vernon asked. "Suddenly I'm not feeling well. We better get back to the house."

"You sure?" Vernon asked. Vincent stood up. "Yeah." He kept looking over at the dance floor.

Vernon was still sitting. "Hold on let me finish this beer right quick."

Damn I wish he would hurry up, Vincent said to himself while Vernon was finishing his beer. A Whitney Houston song, "I Wanna Dance With Somebody (Who Loves Me.)" Vernon slammed his empty bottle down on the counter. "Damn that was good," he said with a smile. "Come on Vernon I'm a sick man and you're stalling."

"Cry baby," Vernon said. They were going out the door. "Hold up, I forgot my keys," Vernon said. He picked up his keys off the bar counter and he happened to see Amber on the dance floor when he looked that direction. "What's the hold up?" Vincent asked, when he over to him. "Amber is here."

"Where?" Vernon pointed her out. "You sure. That might be someone that look like her."

"It's her because I see that no good friend of hers on the dance floor too."

Vernon marched over there to her. Amber was getting down on the dance floor but when she saw Vernon's face, she screamed so loud, everyone stopped and so did the music. Amber felt so embarrassed, she ran out of the club. Amber sat in the passenger's seat of Vernon's car and Vincent was in the back seat. When Vernon got in the car, Amber wouldn't look his way because she knew he was looking at her. Nobody made a sound for a moment. "What the hell is wrong with you? Didn't I tell you to bring your butt right back home?" Amber looked at him. "I'm sorry," she said. "Yeah you're going to be sorry," Vernon said, starting up the car. When they got home, Vernon was undressing still looking seriously at Amber while she was sitting on the bed. "Dancing with another man in the club," he said. "Vernon, Chesna talked me into going there."

"See that's the problem. You are going to stop hanging around that help her for now on. She ain't got no man, you do."

Amber wanted to say something else but chose not to. She gets out of her clothes into her nightgown and goes straight to bed. The next evening Amber just got off work and had Chesna with her. "I really don't want to be over here because I don't like Vernon," Chesna said. "Don't worry he's not here right now," Amber said. "Good I need to use your restroom because I'm about to pee in my pants."

Chesna ran down the hallway, opened the door to the bathroom not knowing Vincent was in there. He was half naked with a towel wrapped around his waist. "Oh I'm sorry…I didn't know anyone was in here."

"That's alright I was on my way out," Vincent said. Chesna peeked around the corner as he was going down the hallway. Amber was sitting in the living room when she came from the bathroom. "Girl who is that beautiful man you have up in here?"

"That is my brother-in-law to be."

"That long curly hair and those muscles. You should be marrying him, not Vernon. But I'm glad you're not because I want him."

"You can't go out with him," Amber said. "Why not? He has a girlfriend or something?"

"I don't know."

"Well I'm taking he's available."

"Time to go home Chesna."

"Oh you kicking me out. That's okay…. I'm going to have some good sleep tonight. Dreaming about the man of my dreams."

Then Vernon comes home. "What the hell are you doing in my house?" Vernon asked. "I'm leaving," Chesna said, giving him a dirty look. Vernon gives her one back. He sits next to Amber, putting his arm around her. "How was work?" he asked. "It was good," Amber answered. "I'm so tired though, I just wanna relax."

"How about we take a shower?" Vernon asked. "I don't want to get my hair wet. I just got it done."

"You won't get your hair wet. Go on, get out of your clothes…I'll be waiting on you."

"Okay," Amber said and she gives him a kiss Amber was sitting at the kitchen table, eating some spaghetti she just made. She hears someone come in the front door. Vincent comes in the kitchen with a woman. "Hey what's up Amber?"

"What's up?"

"Amber this is Tanika, Tanika this is my brother's fiancée, Amber."

"Nice to meet you," Tanika said, shaking Amber's hand. "Same here," Amber said. "I better get going because I have class tonight," Tanika said to Vincent. "You didn't want anything to drink before you leave?" he asked. "No thank you."

"I'll walk you to your car."

"I'll be fine," Tanika said. He sees her to the door. "I'll see you tomorrow," Vincent said. "Sure," she said. Vincent goes back to the kitchen. "You hungry?" Amber asked. "Yeah I'm starving."

Amber gets a clean plate out of the dishwasher and began putting some spaghetti on the plate. "You don't have to do that, I can get it," Vincent said. Amber handed him the plate and she sat back down, eating her spaghetti. Vincent sits across from her with his plate of spaghetti. "What time does Vernon get back home?" he asked. "In a couple of hours."

"Good, this is a good time for us to talk and get to know each other better since we're going to be family."

"Okay," she said. "So are you originally from Tulsa?"

"No I was born and raised in Oklahoma City. I moved here about five years ago."

"Oh what made you move here?"

"I don't know I just like Tulsa better I guess."

"You have any family here?"

"Just a cousin. My folks still stay in Oklahoma City. I have an older brother that lives in Phoenix with his wife and kids."

"Do you have any children?" Vincent asked. "No," Amber answered. "Do you want kids?"

"Yeah I definitely do but I want to wait about three years. I'm going to school his fall to study business. I want to have my own little business, a clothing store."

"That's good I like to see a young black woman wanting to do something with themselves. Have you and my brother discussed all this, like when you guys are going to have kids after you're married?"

"Yes."

"I'm only asking because Vernon was telling me something different."

"Different?" she asked. "Yes he was telling me you were going to quit your job and start having kids right away."

"Really."

"Yes he said it like that's the way it's going to be after you two get married. I know my brother. He's the kind of man that wants things his way. Did you know about his ex-wife, Shantal?"

"No."

"She was just like you, doing good, and going further in life but Vernon was trying to tell her how to live her life. Shantal wasn't going to let him. He wouldn't stop trying to run her life so she left him. I'm not trying to tell you, you shouldn't marry Vernon but you should really think about what I've told you. "You're only…how old are you?"

"Twenty-seven," Amber said. "You have your whole life ahead of you and you have your own mind. Well I'm going to take shower and take a nap. This was some good spaghetti."

"Thank you," Amber said. Vincent put his plate in the sink. "One more thing… Vernon doesn't have to know we had this conversation."

Amber nodded her head. "Alright," Vincent said, smiling. He left the kitchen. Amber began picking at her almost empty plate of spaghetti, thinking Sunday morning, everyone got ready for church. Amber was in the bathroom still getting ready. Vincent and Tanika were sitting on the couch talking while Vernon was pacing back and forth, looking at his watch. "Amber! We need to go!" Vernon screamed. Amber was trying to ignore him. She was just now stepping into her high heels. She wasn't feeling that well because it was that time of the month. Plus she wasn't in no mood for no stuff. "Amber!" Vernon screamed again. She came out of the bathroom. "You don't have to keep shouting my name."

"Well hurry up then," he said. Amber walked passed Vernon on her way out the door. Vernon was just standing there looking at her. She stopped and looked back at him. "Well what are you waiting on?" Amber asked. "Are you two ready?" Vernon asked Vincent and Tanika. "Yeah we're ready," Vincent said. They all got in Vernon's Lexus and headed off to church. Church was really crowded that day and enjoyable. They had prayer, took communion, the choir sung two song selections, and now the sermon. During the sermon, Amber's cramps were kicking her butt. She couldn't sit still. "What's wrong with you?" Vernon asked. "Nothing," Amber answered. Vernon put his arm around her. Vincent had his arm around Tanika. Tanika was getting restless. "This is so boring," Tanika said. "What are you talking about? This a good sermon," Vincent said. "Well I don't like church."

Tanika reached into her purse and pulled out a stick of gum. She started chewing it and popping it. People were looking at her. "Tanika you cannot be chewing gum in church," Vernon said. She rolled her eyes. Vincent pulled out a Kleenex out of his pocket. "I'm not taking this gum out."

"Come on be nice," Vincent said. Tanika took her gum out and put it in the Kleenex. He balled up the Kleenex and put it in his pocket. She started rubbing his thigh. "Stop Tanika we are in church."

"You like that didn't you?"

"Will you please stop talking. I'm trying to hear the word," an old lady sitting in front of them said. "Sorry ma'am," Vincent said They arrived back at the house about two o' clock that afternoon. Amber got a glass of water from the kitchen sink and popped a pill. Then she sat down in the living room. Vincent and Tanika were standing there in the living room talking and laughing. Vernon was in the kitchen looking around. He quickly went back to the living room.

"Aren't you going to cook today?" Vernon asked. Amber stood up. "No I want to go out to eat."

"Out to eat, don't you think you should be cooking?"

"Look I cook about four or five days out of the week. Plus I'm working woman. I'm going out to eat."

Vernon was mad as hell. "You guys coming?" Vernon asked. "No we're going to stay here and order some Chinese food," Vincent said. Vernon and Amber left. "I thought we'd never be alone," Tanika said, putting her arms around Vincent's neck. "Hold on, don't you think we should eat first?"

"No I think we should get down to business first."

"It be best if we ate first so we'll have some energy. Sex is better on a full stomach."

"By the time we get the food and eat, they'll be back," Tanika said. "Then why don't we go to your place?"

"My parents might be home. Come on Vincent give it to me, give it to me right now."

"How about we call the pizza delivery and while we're waiting on the pizza to come, we can be getting our freak on."

"But what if I don't want to stop," she said, getting an attitude. "I think you're just making all these excuses because you don't want to do it to me."

"Well we don't know each other that well."

"What do you want from me?" Tanika asked. "I'm thirty-five year old man, I'm looking for something serious. "I'm serious about having sex right now."

"Tanika please."

"Please my ass! What kind of man turns down pussy? You could be gay for all I know… I'm outta here."

She walks out.

Vincent shakes his head. "Kids these days," he said. Vernon keeps looking at Amber and his menu at the same time. Amber kept her eyes on the menu. She didn't look at him once or said anything since they got to the restaurant. "What are you getting?" he asked. She didn't respond. "Damn it, you're going to talk to me!" Their server came. "Hello I'm Mindy what can I get for you?"

"I'd like the southern fried chicken with mashed potatoes and gravy with a garden salad," Amber said. "What kind of dressing?"

"Ranch."

"Did you want brown or white gravy?" Amber looked at Vernon with a smirk on her face. "White gravy."

He was burning up with anger on the inside. "And for you, sir?" 'I'd like the grilled cod with the mixed vegetables and a Caesar salad."

"Okay anything else?"

"No thank you," Vernon said. She took their menus and said," I'll be right back."

"Why are you trying to be funny?" Vernon asked. "What's funny?" Amber asked. "You know damn well you don't eat white gravy."

"What difference does it make?"

"And fried chicken isn't good for you."

"I'll eat whatever the fuck I want to eat."

"We just got of church and you're using profanity."

"So what."

"What is going on with you Amber?"

"You. I'd appreciate it if you leave me alone."

"Fine you wanna be like that."

They wouldn't speak to each other the whole time until the bill came. Amber slapped her Visa on the table. "Hold on I'll get it. I got cash," Vernon said. "You ready to pay?" Mindy asked. "Yes," Amber answered. She picked up her Visa and handed it to her. "Thank you, be right back."

Vernon put his wallet back in his pocket. Amber knew he had a pist-off look on his face but she refused to look at him. But he kept quiet. Mindy brought back her credit card receipt. Amber signed it and Mindy gave her Visa back. "Thanks you folks have a great day."

"You do the same," Amber said. Amber was walking fast to the car. Vernon grabbed her arm. "Why are you trying so hard to make me look bad?" She pulled her arm out of his hand. "You're making yourself look bad by putting your hands on me."

He got in the car then she got in and they went home. Vernon went straight to the bedroom and shuts the door. Vincent was sitting at the kitchen table, eating a slice of pizza. Amber was getting some water out of the faucet. "You guys enjoyed yourselves?" Vincent asked. Amber didn't say nothing. She just drank her water and went about her business. "I guess they had a great time," Vincent said. When Amber went into their bedroom, Vernon was out of church clothes into some comfortable clothes. She sat on the bed taking off her shoes. Vernon sat on the other side of the bed, looking at a magazine. He was being very quiet. Amber knew he must have been extremely angry with her. She felt bad. "I'm sorry, I didn't mean to be mean."

They weren't looking at each other when she said that. She got up and stood in front of him. "It was just that time of the month. I want to be a good wife. I want to make you happy and I want to be happy. Can I make it up to you? What do you want me to do?"

"I want you to respect me and do what I say…do I make myself clear?"

"Yes," Amber said Memorial Day was coming up so Amber called her mother. "Hi mama how are you?"

"Good how are you doing?" her mother asked. "I'm good. "Are you coming down for Memorial Day weekend? The whole family is going to be here."

"I'm certainly am…. want me to bring anything?"

"Not really but if you want you can."

Vernon just walked in the front door. "Gotta go mama, I can't wait to see everyone."

"Love you hun, bye."

After Amber finished talking to her mother, she ran to Vernon with much excitement. "Vernon my mother wants us to come to Oklahoma City for Memorial Day weekend."

Vernon didn't look excited. "I'm not going and neither are you," he said. "What? Why not?" Amber asked. "Because my family decided to have Memorial Day get together here this year."

"But I told my mother I was coming."

"We went down there last year and all your family could do was look at me strange."

"They just don't really know you yet. Give them time."

"We've been together two years how long does it take to know someone?" he asked. Amber shook her head. "What is your family slow or something?"

"My family doesn't look at you strange."

She goes in the kitchen and Vernon follows her but he sits down at the table and asked, "What's for dinner? "Sunday, the day before Memorial Day, Vincent was in the backyard putting hot dogs, chicken, and hamburgers on the grill. Vernon and Amber were in the kitchen preparing food and setting out paper plates and plastic ware. "Everything should be ready except for the meat and my people should be here soon," Vernon said. "I'm going to change," Amber said. "Put on something sexy," he said. She called down to Oklahoma City when she went in the bedroom. "What happened to you?" her mother asked. "I can't make it," Amber said. "Why?"

"I can't make it."

"It's Vernon isn't it? Ooo I can't stand him and neither can the rest of our family."

"Mama please understand."

"He's understand something when I get a hold of him."

"Mama!"

"Okay if staying there is what you want to do, that's what you should do."

"Tell everyone I'll see them soon."

"Okay bye sweetie," her mother said. Amber was hurt that she couldn't see her family. She showered and put on a tight skimpy dress. Vernon was sitting at the kitchen table when she came back. He had a funny look on his face. "I said to put on something sexy, not that damn sexy."

"What's wrong with this?" Amber asked. "Too revealing. What are you doing wearing something like that anyway?" They heard honking outside. Vernon rushed to the front door. His mother Glenda and his little sister Teely, were getting out of their Ford Escort. Their cousins Shannon and Shawn drove Vincent's '84 Cadillac from Kansas. They all had their children, Teely's two girls, Shannon's boy and Shawn's boy. "What's going on peoples?" Vernon asked. "What's going on with you old man?" Shannon asked. "I'm far from old," Vernon said. They hugged. "Hey little sis."

"What's up?" Teely asked. They hugged. "And how's my nieces and nephews?"

"Hi Uncle Vernon," all the kids said. He kissed his nieces on the forehead. "Now get your bad asses in the house," Vernon said. Vernon was looking at Teely's tight short shorts she had on. "What do you got on?"

"None of your business," she said. "Hey Vernon, where's Vincent?" Shawn asked. "In the backyard."

Shawn went to the backyard and so did the rest of them. Glenda was taking her time coming in the house. "Mama you okay?" Vernon asked. "I'm fine just taking my time."

He kissed her on the cheek. She walked straight to the kitchen and sat at the table. Vernon was looking at the outfit Glenda had on when she was taking a pack of cigarettes out of her purse. "Now what you got on?"

"Shut up and light my damn cigarette!" Vernon picked up a lighter off the kitchen counter and lit her cigarette. "You females are a trip these days. Soon as it gets warm, you want to dress half naked. "Where's my baby Vincent at?" Glenda asked. "Backyard."

She went to the backyard where everyone else was. Vernon went too. While everyone was in the back, Amber had her little suitcase, snuck quietly out of the house and made a clean getaway to Oklahoma City. Glenda was kissing Vincent on the face.

"Mama why do you always be spoiling him?" Vernon asked. "Because I'm special," Vincent said. "That's right. This is my baby," Glenda said. "You Vernon…are an idiot."

"Why I got to be an idiot?"

"You keep changing your wedding date. You just had to change it to the fifteenth. Why couldn't you have kept it on the first? Now we got to make another trip down here."

"Well why don't I do this… I'll come down to Kansas City a couple days before the wedding and I can help you and Teely drive back here."

"You better," Glenda said. "Where's your fiancée at?' Shannon asked. "Good question," Vernon said. Vernon went in the house. "Amber!" he called. He looked all over the house. She was nowhere to be found. Amber made it to Oklahoma City in less than two hours. Amber's brother, Eric answered the door. "Amber!"

"Eric!" They hugged. "Look everyone…Amber's here!"

"Amber… I thought you couldn't make it" her mother, Angie Mae, said. "I managed to get away," Amber said. Her mother hugged her. "I'm glad you made it."

Everyone was sitting around eating and watching the movie "The Color Purple."

Amber's father, Clayton and some uncles of hers were playing dominos in the kitchen. "Hi daddy," she said when she put her arm around him."

"Hey baby girl," he said still into the game. "Hey Charles and Mickie."

"What's going on?" Charles asked. "Are you Angie Mae asked. "Yes."

"Help yourself. We've got plenty of food. Amber fixed herself a plate and watched TV with everyone else. When the movie was over, everyone went outside to play volleyball. They played for hours. All the relatives that came from out of town, went back to their hotels at the end of the day, exhausted. Clayton went to bed, Amber helped Angie Mae clean up the kitchen. "How's everything in Tulsa?"

"Good I guess."

"You guess?" Angie Mae asked. "Mama I'm having doubts about marrying Vernon."

"Praise the Lord. I don't want you to marry that fool anyway."

"I think he wants to control my life."

"It's your choice on what you want to do but my suggestion is you should leave him. You're too young to be throwing your life away."

Tears filled Amber's eyes. Angie Mae held her. "I know you want to get married now but there's a better man out there for you."

Amber came back to Tulsa early Tuesday evening. It looked like no one was home. Vernon's car and Vincent's sar was there but there was some lights left on in the house. Amber unpacked her suitcase in the bedroom. Then she took a shower and she put on her bathrobe when she went back to the bedroom. Amber stood in front of the mirror combing her damp hair. In the mirror she saw Vernon standing in the doorway. He had his hands in his pockets, staring at her. "Why did you leave like that?" he asked. Still looking at him in the mirror she said, "I wanted to see my family."

"You didn't go see your family. Not with that skimpy outfit you had on."

"Yes I did."

"Who's the guy you went to go see?" Vernon asked. "I didn't go see a guy."

"I don't think you went to see your family because you wouldn't of snuck out."

"You didn't want me to go."

"That still doesn't mean you have to sneak out."

"Look I don't want to argue. I want to finish drying off and relax." Amber tried walking past Vernon but he grabbed and pinned her faced down on the bed. He pinned one of her arms behind her back.

"You're going to start listening to me!"

"You're hurting me!" Amber screamed. She started crying, "please!" Vernon let her go and left the room. Amber was still crying and was filled with fear. An hour later, Amber went to bed but couldn't go to sleep. Vernon got into bed with her. Amber turned the other way. "You had no right to do me like that," she said. "I know it wasn't right but you have to stop trying to make me mad."

No one said anything for a moment. Do you still want to get married?" Vernon asked. "Not if you continue to man handle me."

"I'm not trying to man handle you. Listen next week I'm going to Kansas City, Kansas for a couple of days then I'm coming back with my mother and sister in time for our wedding. We're going to have a big wedding. All of my family and your family."

"Why did you push back the wedding date?" Amber asked.

"Because I wanted to."

"How can you say that? You never discuss anything with me."

"You mean everything to me Amber…I'm glad you're in my life."

A week and a half later, Vernon was packed up, ready to head to Kansas City. Vincent was in his Cadillac waiting to drive him to the bus station. Amber walked with Vernon to the door. He took her by the hand. "Vincent is going to stay here and look after you. I really hate being away from you." He kissed her. "I love you," Vernon said. He picked up his suitcase and headed out.

Amber closed the door behind him. Friday evening, Chesna came by. Vincent was sitting on the couch when Amber came rushing to the door to in her heels. "I got it," Amber said. She let Chesna in. "You two look nice…. Where you heading to?" Vincent asked. A friend of ours from work is having a party at her house," Amber said. Chesna sits next to Vincent with a really big smile on her face. "You look really good Vincent. What are you into tonight?"

"I don't know. I'll probably get a drink or something."

"What about after I leave the party? Can we do something?"

"We'll see," Vincent said. "Girl you are silly. I'm going to get my purse," Amber said. "Is that your Cadillac out there?"

"Yep," he said. "You going to take me for a ride in it one day?" Chesna asked. "Sure I don't have a problem with that."

Next thing someone was banging on the front door. Vincent answered it. It was Tanika, all dressed up. "What are you doing here?" Vincent asked. "I came to see you and to apologize. Vincent stepped outside. Chesna wanted to be nosy so when she stepped outside on the porch, she saw Tanika with her arms around Vincent. "Wait just a minute!" Chesna screamed, pulling Tanika's hands off of him. "Who the hell are you?" Tanika asked. Chesna pressed her body against Vincent and squeezed him tight. "I'm his woman and you're not about to steal my hunk of chocolate."

Vincent's mouth was hanging open. "Chesna why don't you go back inside and wait for me."

"Yeah go back inside better yet, leave!" Tanika said. Chesna gave Tanika a look and said," I don't want to go back inside."

"Please for me," he said. "Okay only because you asked me to."

Chesna stood inside, right by the door so she could hear what they're talking about. "What's going on?" Amber asked Chesna. "Shhh," Chesna said. "Why are you with hoodrat?" Tanika asked Vincent. "No, she did not call me a hoodrat" Chesna said. "What's it to you anyway? You went off on me and walked out on that one Sunday afternoon remember?" Chesna and Amber came out. "We gotta go so I'll see you later," Chesna said to Vincent.

She rolled her eyes at Tanika when she walked past her. "Can I come inside so we can talk?" Tanika asked. "Oh, so you want to talk or do want to have sex? It's Friday night and I don't want to do either one with you." Vincent goes inside and shuts the door in her face.

Tanika slowly walks to her car drives away. Lindsey brought Amber and Chesna back to Amber's place at two in the morning. Amber got out of the car. Chesna was laying in the back seat because she was too drunk to drive home. "Amber tell Vincent I'll have to get with another time," Chesna said. "I'm sure he'll understand… have a good night," Amber said. "Same to you," Lindsey said. She sped off. Amber went into the dark house. She headed for the kitchen, then turned on the light. Vincent was sitting at the table with a half empty beer bottle. "Oh, Vincent you scared me…. Why are you sitting in the dark?"

"No reason. Guess what I found me an apartment."

"That's good."

"For under three hundred a month. I'll be moving out next week. I know you two would like your privacy since you're about to get married."

Amber sighs. "I'm not going to marry Vernon. I just made up my mind. He doesn't treat me the way I want to be treated."

"I agree with you. I love my brother, but he can be cold."

"I was going to leave before he got back but I think it would be appropriate to wait until he comes back "Are you positively sure you want to leave him?"

"Yes. Vernon did ask me a week ago did I still want to get married but I didn't give him a definite answer. I should of told him then but what difference would it have made, he wouldn't have listened anyway."

"Yeah you deserve better."

They stared at each other. Vincent stood up. "I really want to tell you something," he said. "The day I moved in, I liked you. On how you wanted me to feel at home. No woman has ever made me feel that way."

"You and Vernon are so different. Vernon is controlling and you're so laid back."

"You just got with the wrong brother when you could get with the right one."

He placed one of his hands on her cheek and kissed her. They continued to kiss. Then she pulled away."

"You know, Chesna really likes you."

"I really like you," Vincent said. "I'm not saying you should get with me because I don't want my brother coming after me from stealing his woman. I'm going to pray for you. I pray you find someone that will treat you the way you deserve to be treated and I pray I'll find a woman like you."

They put they're arms around each other and kissed again. Then he looked in to her eyes. "What just happened is going to be our little secret," he said. "Our little secret," Amber agreed.

It was five in the morning, three hours later since she and Vincent had kissed. Amber was lying in bed thinking about it. It made her hot. His kiss was different from Vernon's. Vernon's kisses were like short boring, dry kisses. Vincent's was so seductive, it took you to another world. She was so worried about how Vernon was going to react towards her not wanting to marry him. He was coming back today with his mom, sister, and some other relatives. They're going to be pissed that they came here for nothing, Amber knew she was in for it Saturday high noon, Amber just got through fixing herself up. Thirty minutes later, Vernon, Teely, and Glenda pulled up in front. "Vincent they're here!" Amber called out. Amber and Vincent stood in the living room waiting on them to come in and she was shaking a little bit. "You alright?" Vincent asked. "I'm fine."

Her voice was shaky too. You certainly are fine, Vincent thought to himself, staring at her hard. Vincent hugged his mom and sister as soon as they walked in the door. Vernon dropped his suitcase on the floor. "I hate over the road riding or driving," he said. Vernon took one look at Amber and forgot about everyone else. "Baby you look…you look so good." He took her by the hand. "Look at you glowing…what kind of lipstick is that you have on?"

"Red Auburn."

"That looks sexy on you." He moved close to her to get a kiss. "No Vernon, not…now."

"Okay later when we're alone," Vernon said. "Better yet we should save all the lovin' for our honeymoon. For days in Miami for our honeymoon. Do you like the sound of that? All the fun we're going to have under the sun and every night in the hotel."

"Don't talk like that in front of me," Glenda said. "Hello Amber, we missed you the last time."

Yeah I had to leave for a moment."

"So, are you ready to marry Mr. Boss man?" Teely asked. Amber was hesitating to answer. "Yeah…Vernon can we talk in private?" Vernon and Amber went into the kitchen. "Vincent, I mean Vernon…I haven't been…feeling okay----- You're pregnant? I knew you was." He gave her a big hug. "You don't have to worry about anything. I'm going to take care you and our child and you won't have to do anything."

Vernon went back into the living room. "We have a little one on the way."

"Wow you two didn't waste time," Glenda said. "I'm going to have another little niece or nephew!" Teely said, with excitement. Vincent said nothing. Amber was still in the kitchen, thinking this man does not want to listen. Later that day, some more family members of Vernon and Vincent's, including their father, Ted showed up. Afterwards they all went out to eat. Vernon announced to other family members that didn't know yet that he and Amber were about to have their first child. Everyone was happy for them. "Be sure to eat extra food because I want to have a healthy grandson," Ted said. "How do you know it will be a boy…it might be a girl," Glenda said. Next thing, them two started fussing. Amber just wanted to scream. Amber and Vincent was sitting across from each other and was just staring at each other while everyone else was just talking, and talking, and talking….All their family members checked in their hotel rooms that night. Vernon went straight to sleep. Amber didn't want to sleep so she went outside. She looked up at the half moon, wandering how she was getting out of this one. Vincent had just pulled up in the driveway. Amber walked towards him when he got out of his car. "Is everything alright?" he asked. "I just couldn't tell him no…he wouldn't let me anyway and I never told him I was pregnant."

Vernon turned over in bed trying to feel for Amber. He got up and walked through the house. Vernon noticed the front door was opened.

He looked through the screen door and saw Amber and Vincent standing real close like they was about to kiss, with her hands in his. Vernon may have been half asleep but he knew what he saw. He hurried back to the bedroom and laid back down --- on fire. Sunday morning, Vernon was sitting on the edge of the bed with his chin rested on his knuckles. He was still in his pajamas but then he put on a T-shirt and some jeans. Amber has been in the bathroom since she woke up. Vincent was still in his room. Vernon didn't know if his brother was still asleep or not because his door was shut, so he knocked on his door. Vincent opens the door and was in a suit. "Can I talk to you?" Vernon asked. "Sure," answered. Vernon saw that he packed up all his clothes and other things of his. "How come you're not dressed yet?" Vincent asked. "Vincent you're my brother and I never thought I would be asking you this question…why are you trying to mess around with my woman behind my back?"

"What are you talking about?"

"I think you know after what I saw last night."

"Amber doesn't want to marry you."

"That's not a good enough reason."

"She doesn't feel you treat her right and neither do I."

"I see… you still trying to be the mack."

"I ain't trying to be no mack."

"Come on Vincent. You and I both know you don't never turn down sex."

Amber peeked out the bathroom, listening to their conversation. A knock was at the front door. Ted, Glenda, Teely, and other family members were all dressed up and ready. Everybody made themselves comfortable in the living room after Amber let them in. "How are you on this June day?" Glenda asked," and where is Vernon and Vincent?"

"There's sort of a problem," Amber said. "A problem…that's not good," Ted said. Vernon and Vincent were still in the room having their brotherly love conversation. "So how long you've been sleeping with her?"

"You're crazy we have never slept together."

"Lately she's been calling me Vincent. I should of known then."

"I've never touched her."

"You had to have done something."

"Well maybe we kissed."

"You did or you did not kiss?"

"Yes, Vernon we kissed, only once."

"Man, it must have been one hell of a kiss for a woman to call a man another man's name. Amber doesn't really want to leave me. You've just filled her head with things. This all happening because someone's trying to make a fool out of me on my wedding day."

"You're the one starting something," Vincent said. "Yeah because you were all in my fiancée's face last night."

"It wasn't meant for you to get married today."

"Who the heck are you?"

"Your brother," Vincent answered. "What's all this yelling about back here?" Glenda asked when she walked in. Vernon walked out of the room. Glenda and Vincent, was right behind him. He stood in the middle of the living room, facing Amber, with everyone's attention on them. Vernon had his arms folded. "Do you or do you not want to get married?" he asked. "No, I don't. You want to know why, Vernon?" He was waiting for an answer. "Because you don't listen, you don't care about my wants or needs and I certainly don't appreciate you telling your family that I'm pregnant. I don't like words put in my mouth."

"So, what are you saying?"

"It's over."

Vernon stared at Amber for a long time with anger rising in him. Then he walked away. Glenda grabbed his arm. "Where are you going?"

"Just leave me alone! Everyone get out of my house!" Vernon snatched his arm from her and went into his bedroom then locked the door behind himself. Glenda, Vincent, and Teely stood outside of his door. "Vernon please come out. Let's talk about this," Glenda said. Vernon wouldn't respond. Ted boarded to the door. "Vernon bring your ass out here!" They still didn't get a response. The other family members were still in the living room, confused about what was going on. All of a sudden, they heard a loud bang. Everybody was quiet. "What was that?" Teely asked. "Vernon!" Vincent called, beating on the door. "Vernon baby please open the door," Glenda said. Nobody could open the door so Vincent got a hammer from under the kitchen sink and broke the door knob. When they all went in the room, Vernon was laying on the floor with his shirt soaked with blood. A gun was lying next to him. Glenda and Teely started crying. Ted and Vincent were stunned. Amber came into the room, saw what happened, and cried too. Instead of a wedding that day, everyone spunt their time at the hospital. The good news was that Vernon was going to survive. Vincent and Amber believed Vernon shot himself to make the both of them feel guilty but Vincent knew he wasn't crazy enough to kill himself. Nobody could see him that day. Everyone had to come back the next day to see him. Amber didn't, she moved on. Four months later, Amber was sitting down eating her chicken teriyaki sandwich at the food court inside the Woodland Hills Mall. She just got off of work at her new job at the Foley's department store. Amber was about to eat her last bite of her sandwich when someone said, "Hello pretty lady."

She almost choked when she saw it was Vernon. "How you been?" he asked, sitting down across from her. "I've been great, how about you?"

"I've been alright. My mother stays with me now."

"Oh, that's good."

"You stay around here?" Vernon asked. "Yes."

"Are you staying with someone?"

"Why Vernon?"

"I'm sorry, just asking."
He stared at her. "Amber I'm sorry for all things that happened between us."

"I'm sorry too."

"Is there any chance we could start seeing each other again?"

"No, I have to live my life the way I want to live it. I have a better job and I'm going to school now."

He took her hand and kissed it. "I'm proud of you." He stood up. "It was nice seeing you again," she said when he was about to walk away.

'I'll always be thinking about you no matter what," he said. He smiled at her in a way she'll always remember.

The Water Is Still Running

Amber double checked her suitcase, making sure she had everything she needed for her four- day vacation in Los Angeles. "My sun tan lotion, can't forget that."

It was lying up under her two- piece bathing suit. Amber could remember the first time she went to LA, less than ten years ago. She went to see the Jacksons in concert with her cousin. That was a memory. This time around it was just an end of the summer vacation with her best friend Chesna. They wanted to take this trip for the fourth of July holiday but didn't have their money saved up in time. Amber's Indian boyfriend, Jadu came up behind her. "I'm gonna miss you while you're gone."

"Don't worry I'll be back before you know it, but I'm gonna miss you too."

"You're not going to miss me. You're going to have so much fun in the sun."

The doorbell rings. She rushes to the door, then looks through the peep hole and then opens the door. "Ready lady?" Chesna asked. "Yes, more than ready."

Amber goes to grab her suitcase that was on the couch. Chesna waves and said," hello," to Jadu. He said hello back. After she closes up her suitcase, she hugs Jadu and gives him a quick kiss. "Have fun," he said. Chesna's boyfriend Trent, was waiting in the car to drive them to the airport. After they got in the car, they both yelled, "LA here we come!" They arrived at the LAX airport by mid-afternoon. They made way through the crowded airport to the outdoors to catch a taxi to their hotel. Chesna wanted to get a rent-a-car but she wasn't so sure about driving in such a fast pace city even though she was a fast driver. Amber certainly wasn't going to take a chance. They took the taxi to the Comfort Inn Hotel, nearby. Once they got settled in, they were ready to hit the beach. They caught the city bus there. They found the perfect spot in the sand to sit and watch all the action on Venice Beach. Chesna took out her portable radio and tuned it in on a good station. Neneh Cherry's hit "Buffalo Stance" just came on. Amber put on her sunglasses and then rubbed her sun tan lotion on.

"I don't know why you're doing that," Chesna said. "Why am I doing what?" Amber asked. "Putting on sun tan lotion."

"I'm not trying to get dark."

"You are light-skinned. You have a long way to get dark," Chesna said. "I'm beige," Amber said. "During winter you're lighter than what you are now."

"You should be putting this on. You don't need to be getting darker."

"I'm alright, I'm going to search for some hot chocolate brothers."

"You have a man already."

Two white guys were walking past them. They looked and smiled. Amber smiled back. She lowered her sunglasses to get a better look. "There's certainly isn't nothing wrong with looking."
"You have a man too and you're looking."

"Just looking at a double scoop of vanilla ice cream. "You have that gorgeous Native Indian."

"I know, but I don't know about us."

"What are you talking about?"

"We're just too… different. We don't have much in common. It seems lately I haven't had much in common with anybody."

"You know Trent has been trying to find a good barber to go to since his brother won't cut his hair anymore. Guess where he gets his haircuts now? Vernon's."

Amber didn't respond. "You mean you're really over him? Every time we go into Vernon's shop, he looks unhappy all the time. He never says a word to me though."

Amber gets up and walks towards the water. She stands in the water while it hits her up to her ankles. Amber stares out into the great Pacific Ocean. Chesna squatted down beside Amber, putting her hands in the water. "Maybe I can find some seashells."

Amber yanked her foot making Chesna fall back on her chunky butt. Chesna looked up at her. A sudden smile came to Amber's face. Chesna grabbed her leg. Amber fell back flat in the water. They busted out a laugh. They made the best of their trip, to Universal Studios, to shopping, to Hollywood, taking pictures of all the stars names they could on the Hollywood walk of fame. When it was time to head back home. Amber napped on the plane and was thinking she needed to vacation more. Amber returns home Monday afternoon. Her apartment seemed so peaceful. *Jadu must be napping because his car was still there* When she headed for her bedroom, Amber heard talking from her room.

The door was closed but not completely shut. She slowly pushed the door opened. Her boyfriend, another guy and two women were sitting on her bed sharing a needle. "What the hell!" Amber screamed. They all were startled. "Jadu… who are these people?"

"You back so soon?" Jadu said. "Cut the bull you knew I was coming back today. Get out of my house."

The guy and the women left. "That includes you too," she to Jadu. "Let me explain."

"How dare you do something like this in my house. I want you out now!" He leaves. Amber still couldn't believe what she just seen but she had to calm herself and tell herself it's just Monday Chesna met Amber at her job when it was time for her to get off. Amber worked in the cosmetic department at Foley's in Woodland Hills Mall. Amber was walking so fast, Chesna had to walk faster to keep up with her. "Can I ask how your day was?" Chesna asked. "It was okay I just have a lot on my mind and I'm just ready to eat."

"Yeah forget him. He should of known better," Chesna said. When they got to the food court, Chesna went for pizza.

Amber stood next to a table, looking around not knowing what she really wanted. Someone called her name. It was a man's voice. When she turned to look, she couldn't believe it. "Vincent!"

"It's been a long time," he said. "Yeah," Amber said. They shook hands. She couldn't get over how good he looked. He still had a jheri curl but it was cut lower and he had a beard now. His attire was so pimped out he looked like a billionaire. His suit was silver with pin stripes and the material was silk. His tie and shirt went with it perfectly. His silver watch and his gray snake skin shoes topped it off. Amber was taking in a whiff of his cologne. He was looking so good and smelling so good she wanted to throw him on the table and have him for dinner. Chesna came back with her pizza and soda. "You decided what you're going to… "Oh Chesna you remember Vernon's brother, Vincent?" She stared at him so hard she forgot what Amber asked her. "Oh yes…I remember."

"It's great to see you," Vincent said to Chesna. "What brings you to the mall?" Amber asked. "I'm here with my fiancée."

"Fiancée," Amber said. "Yeah here she comes now. Amber and Chesna couldn't believe it. His fiancée was short, older looking than him, she also had a jheri curl that was shoulder length and had a dark burgundy colored dress on. "Hey honey," she said. Vincent introduced her to Amber and Chesna . "Nice to meet you," she said. "Same here," Amber said. "Vincent I'm going to get me something to eat, you want something?"

"Whatever you're getting," he said. "Okay I'll be back."

He kissed her on the cheek before she walked away. "So, when's the wedding?" Amber asked. "We haven't set a date, yet but I'll let you know but I gotta go. See you ladies around."

"Bye," Amber said. "He looks so good," Chesna said. "but I'm not going to their wedding."

"Why?"

"That old thing is marrying the man of my dreams."

"Chesna let it go. Seeing him made my day better though," Amber said. "Now I need something to eat… maybe some McDonald's."

Second day back from out of town and I get surprises, Amber said to herself lying on her bed watching TV alone. What next? I might run into Vernon. He's probably married, settled down by now. I don't know. Chesna says when she sees him, he never looks happy. I know I need to meet the right one. I'm almost thirty, a new decade is approaching… why haven't I found somebody? Maybe because I've been settling for less these past two years. I really wonder how Vernon's doing. I know… I can pay him a visit at his shop tomorrow evening. He's the only guy on earth I know a lot about other than the men in my family. I've haven't seen him in two years. In this small city I haven't ran into him not once. So, tomorrow evening…I'm looking forward to Vernon's shop closes at six. Amber got off work at five thirty so she rushed there. All his employees had just left but Vernon's Lexus was still there. He was closing up when she went inside. She said, "hi" when he seen her. "Amber." He walked over to her and gave her a hug. "Have a seat."

She sat in one of the chairs the customers sit in. He comes around and kisses her on the forehead. Then he sits next to her. "So, what brings you by?"

"I just decided to pay you a visit."

"So, what you've been doing?" Vernon asked. "Just working."

"Where you work at?"

"At Foley's in the Woodland Hills Mall."

He didn't say nothing for a moment. He took a moment to look her over. "You look really nice."

"Thank you."

"I was going to get something to eat, you want to come with me?" Vernon asked. "Maybe next time. I have things to get done at home."

"You have a number I can reach you at?" he asked. "Yes."

Amber pulled out a pen and a scratch pad out of her purse. She wrote her number down, then handed the piece of paper to him. "I'll call you when I get home."

"I'll be waiting for your call."

He walked her to her car. Vernon really wanted to talk about some things. It made Amber was eager to get home, so she can be there ready. Vernon called Amber around seven-thirty. He wanted her to stop by his place tomorrow night. Amber insisted to wait until the weekend to come by. "That would be better," he agreed. After she got off the phone with him, Amber was thinking, I'm glad he agreed to see me over the weekend because it shows he doesn't have anyone living with him, but it doesn't mean he's not seeing anybody. I'm certainly not falling back into the life I once had with him, that's a promise. Amber got off work at nine then arrived at Vernon's house at nine-thirty Saturday night. She knew he had to be cooking because the smell of food filled the place. Something he's never done when they was together. He also had Stephanie Mills playing on the radio. "I'm so glad you dressed up for this occasion," he said. "Thanks, I'm glad too. I see you dressed for it too."

"Yep," he said. "Come with me, I'm going to show you what I'm cooking."

He had salmon baking in the oven. He had just finished cooking some green beans and dressing. Vernon also had some dinner rolls that were done sitting on top of the stove and a seven-up cake. The kitchen table was set with two plates, silverware, two plastic cups and a big pitcher of sweet tea sliced lemons floating in it. "Wow I'm impressed. I'm going to go to the bathroom and wash my hands. He nodded. Amber washed her hands and made sure she looked alright in the mirror. She almost forgot how to get to the bathroom since it's been so long since she's been here. Amber made sure they prayed over their food before eating. She had second helpings. Vernon just had another salmon. After they finished their dinner, they went to the living room to look at some TV. Amber sat her half cup of sweet tea on the little table in front of them. "You liked everything?" he asked. "Definitely."

"I could tell. You ate quite a bit."

"It feels strange being back here, since it's been two years I've been here."

"I've kept everything the same," Vernon said. "You have a boyfriend?"

"No."

"Cute as you are, and you have no one?"

"I recently got out of a relationship," Amber said. "I've been wanting to know if you're involved with someone?"

"I have a couple of lady friends but nothing serious. These women out here are driving me crazy. Some have personal issues or too much drama in their life. I've been miserable without you Amber. We should of never broke up."

"We probably wouldn't have if you discussed our future as husband and wife with me."

No one said nothing for a moment. "My brother Vincent is getting married. I think the woman he's marrying is older than he is."

"Really," Amber said, sounding surprised. She dared not to let Vincent's name come out of her mouth because of the shocking incident that occurred over she and Vincent's intimate moment two years ago. "I care about you a lot," she said. "Well we should do something about that, like get back together," Vernon said.

"I want a man that stands behind what I want to do with my life. Not someone who thinks they're going to make decisions without my consent."

"I'm sorry for how I've been," Vernon said. "I've forgiven you a long time ago. Oh, look at the time…I gotta go."

"Why? I was hoping you'd stay the night. We can watch a Prince movie or something."

"I have to get up for church in the morning."

"Oh, how about some cake then?" he asked. Amber and Chesna went to the Rib Crib and brought the barbecue back to Chesna's place after church. "Me and Trent been talking about marriage."

"That's good news," Amber said, trying to eat her ribs. "There's somebody out there for you too, just wait and see."

"I'm almost thirty I don't have forever to wait."

She wasn't going to tell Chesna she's been talking to Vernon. She doesn't know if she wants to rekindle anything with Vernon anyway. So, she still considered herself single. "Good things come to those that wait," Chesna said. "I've waited," Amber said. The next three days Amber has been working ten hour shifts. She loves her job and she loves helping women look beautiful for their husbands, boyfriends or even themselves. Vernon had called her on a Wednesday night. "How come you haven't been calling me or coming by?"

"I've been busy working."

"I don't like it when you don't talk to me."

"Can we talk about this tomorrow? I'm off and right now I want to soak my feet."

"Well I work tomorrow," he said. "Tomorrow evening I mean?" she asked. Vernon didn't say nothing for a second. "You paid me a visit after two freaking years and this is how you want to do me?"

"I haven't done anything to you. If you want us to talk, you can't be acting like this."

Vernon said nothing. "I will certainly call you tomorrow about six," Amber said. "Ok six," he agreed She calls him Thursday evening at six thirty. "How was your day?" Amber asked. "Busy. So, what did you do today since you were off?"

"Nothing really. Clean my apartment, did laundry, cooked.."

"What did you cook?"

"I just fried some chicken, had some mash potatoes and gravy."

"Are you doing anything now?"

"No."

"Why don't you come by here?" Vernon asked. "I can't right now I'm soaking in my bathtub and I'm getting drunk in it."

"Why don't I come over there, I could use a little soak and we could soak together."

"I don't want you knowing where I stay at. Least not yet."

"Don't treat me like a stranger because I'm not one."

"I know."

"Well get yourself down here so I can show you how much I missed you."

"I'm too drunk to drive silly. You want to see me tomorrow?" Amber asked. "I wanna see you right now."

"I'm getting out of the tub, hold on."

She laid the receiver down on the closed lid, toilet so she could dry off. She rubbed some Jergen's lotion all over real, quick She left the bathroom with the phone, straight to her bedroom. "Hello," she said when she was back on the phone. "What was you doing?" he asked. "I had to dry off and rub myself down with some lotion."

"Are you still naked?"

"Yes."

"If I was there I'd bang the mess out of you. What are you about to put on?"

"A short night gown, see-through and my panties are too." "Ohhh you're turning me on."

"I have to go but I'll see you tomorrow night?"

"Only under one condition," he said, "that you spend the whole weekend with me."

"That's no problem, I can do that."

"Okay I want an answer," Chesna said when she stopped by Amber's place after church service. "Why weren't you at church today?"

"No reason," Amber said with a smile. "I was just up too late last night."

"Watching movies?" Chesna asked. "No."

"I hope you weren't out in the streets doing nothing bad."

"Nope. More like nasty."

"Nasty…I don't understand."

"I do," Amber said. Then she starts singing "I'm a nasty girl in my own little nasty world or my name is not Janet but it's Amber if you're nasty."

"Girl what's gotten into you?"

"Vernon."

Chesna went into shock. "Did you say Vernon?"

"Yep."

"Oh no why Amber, why? All the men in the world why him?"

"He was my fiancé, once upon a time. Besides, I haven't been having any luck with anybody else."

"He was also once upon a time a rude and possessive person."

"I just wanted to give him another chance. He was the only that's ever done anything for me."

"Let's just pray he's a different man," Chesna said A month passes by and things between Amber and Vernon have went well liked she hoped. Amber went to church one Sunday without Chesna because she had a cold. She was going to make sure she stopped by the store after church service to get some chicken noodle soup for her friend. When Amber was shaking hands, and got a few hugs from people on her way out the door, someone called her name. "Wow I'm surprised to see you," she said to Vincent. It was a shock to her to see him dressed down in nothing but jeans, T-shirt and tennis shoes.

"How's it going?" Amber asked. "Okay," he answered. "So, where's your fiancée I assume?"

"We're not together anymore."

"Oh, that's too bad."

"You mind if we talk somewhere if only you don't have somewhere to be?" Vincent asked. "I have time."

Amber wanted to eat at a Burger King for a change. She needed a break from cooking at home.

"We broke up two weeks ago," Vincent said after taking a bite of his whopper. "You guys seemed so happy the last time I saw you."

"I thought we were happy too. I found out that she was still married and still seeing him."

"How did you find this out?"

"Ever since we got engaged, she's been sneaking off places and making secretive phone calls which made me suspicious. I followed her one day to her current husband's house. She didn't come out until forty-five minutes later. I questioned her about everything."

"What was her answer?"

"She says they've been discussing over their divorce. I think they've been plotting to get a hold of my money."

"Why you think that?"

"I heard her phone conversations. They're both broke anyway. You should see the house he lives in."

"I'm sorry things haven't worked out for you."

"I don't think I'll ever find Mrs. Right."

"You shouldn't give up Vincent. "I'm almost forty years old. I haven't had a steady relationship in years. I might as a well face it…I'm going to be spending the rest of my life alone."

"You are a great looking guy and I don't understand. I would of thought women would throw themselves at your feet. I don't know you well, but I think you probably have a good heart too."

"That's just it. I'm too nice and too gullible. Nobody likes nice people these days. "I do," Amber said, smiling at him. Vincent smiles back. They were gazing into each other's eyes, the thought of the last time crossed Amber's mind. "I got to get to the store. Chesna's feeling a little under the weather and I need to get her some soup."

"Well tell Chesna I hope she feels better."

"I will."

They shook hands. "We'll talk more sometime," Amber said. Vincent nodded. Vincent was browsing in Foley's on a Friday night. He ended up running into Amber. "Hi, how are you doing?" Amber asked. "Good. Just searching for something new for the weekend…you leaving?" he asked because he saw she still had on her name tag but had her purse. "Yeah, I'm done for the day. I've been here since ten-thirty this morning."

"What are you getting into tonight," Vincent asked. Amber was hesitant to tell. "Just getting changed out of these clothes…for now."
"Oh, if you're not doing anything, would you like to come by my place or I could come by your place."

"Actually Vincent, I do have plans."

"Oh, with your boyfriend or something? I didn't think to ask if you had one. Sorry about that."

"That's okay."

"I still hope we can talk sometime," he said. "Yeah, we definitely can," Amber said. "See you later."

Vincent waved He followed her to Vernon's house. Vincent watched her go in the house when Vernon let her in. He made sure he stayed out of view, but it didn't matter if they seen him. Vincent stared at his brother's house as it started raining and the rain, splashed on the windows of his car. Vernon's mom Glenda and sister Teely drove in from Kansas City, Kansas early Saturday morning. "You back with Amy now?" Teely asked. "Her name is Amber," Vernon said. "When is Vincent suppose to get married?" Glenda asked. "He's not getting married now."

"Why not?"

"He just isn't."

"What is it with you guys? You want to spend the rest of your life by yourself? You or Vincent aren't that young. At least us older folks know how to stay married. "You and daddy aren't together anymore."

"We're still married. We're just separated."

"At least I'm married and live with my husband," Teely said. "Do you have all of what you need for this family gathering?" Glenda asked. "Not yet. Amber's getting a list together and you both can go with her to get the stuff."

"Good I need to get some cigarettes anyway."

"You need to stop smoking," Vernon said. "I'll smoke if I want to smoke."

"Amber should be ready in a second. I want you girls to hurry back because I want to get this party started by five o'clock."

"Well we're going to stop by Vincent's before we go to the store," Glenda said. "Well me and Amber are going to the store and you two go over to Vincent's."

"Fine by me," Glenda said Vernon's eighteen-year-old son, Willy and his girlfriend were the first to arrive at Vernon's house. Then Vernon's dad Ted and Glenda. Teely and her husband Charlie and their two kids. Their cousins Shannon and Shawn and a few other relatives. The last person to show was Vincent, who always had to make a good impression at special occasions. Vernon and Amber had done the cooking. Glenda and Teely helped with some of it. They cooked quite a bit, it was lots left over. Everybody sat around conversating. Amber finished up her food, quietly listening to everyone else. She tossed her paper plate in the kitchen trash when she was finished. Then Amber went down the hall to the bathroom, so she could wash all the barbecue sauce off her hands. Just when she finished washing her hands, someone said, "hello Amber."

She saw Vincent behind her in the mirror. Amber turned around. He was leaning in the doorway with his hands in his pockets. He looked like he just stepped off a Jet magazine cover. Amber dried her hands off on a towel hanging on the wall by the sink. "We haven't had a chance to speak to each other since we've both been here," Vincent said. "Yeah, I've been busy in the kitchen," she said. "You're such a workaholic. You need a massage, a back rub."

He shut the bathroom door and locked it. Vincent eased himself closer to Amber, and she ended up pinned against the wall. "Why did you lock the door?"

"So, we can talk. It's too noisy out there. We won't be able to hear each other."

He pressed his body against hers. "Let me make your body feel at ease." He tried to kiss her, but she turned her head. "Why are you doing this Vincent? Vernon is your brother and you know what happened the last time."

"I know. All I want you to do is touch this." He tried to get her to touch his penis. She pushed him away. "You stay away from me, you dirty-minded creep. Your brother has a house full of family members and you do this."

Amber goes straight to Vernon. "I gotta get going I'm going out with Chesna tonight."

"You're coming back later, right?" Vernon asked. "Yes. I won't be out late" Amber said good-bye to everyone. She was glad to get out of there. She was not having a second time around incident all over again. Amber, Chesna, and their two other friends, Lindsey and Lisa held their wine glasses up to toast Chesna on her thirtieth birthday. "How does it feel to be thirty now?" Lisa asked after they all sipped their wines. "I feel like I reached a new level. It's like back when I turned twenty-one. I've officially became a lady, now I'm a woman and I'm not allowing any man to tell me any different."

"Amen to that," Lindsey said. "Amber's going to be celebrating her thirtieth soon," Chesna said. "And I'm not looking forward to it," Amber said. "You should be. It's a new level of womanhood."

"Excuse me I need to go to the restroom."

Amber goes to the ladies' room. After she came from the stall a minute later, Amber recognized the lady washing her hands at the sink. When she and Vincent's ex-fiancée looked at each other, the lady gave Amber a quick smile then left the bathroom. Amber walked past the table the ex was seated at. An old woman was with her. Amber was sure it was probably her mother. Amber went back to her seat and her friends were eating their lobsters and shrimp dinners that were delivered while she was in the bathroom. "Chesna, remember Vincent's fiancée?"

"Yeah," Chesna said. "She's here? Without him?"

"Yes. Vincent told me they broke up recently. "She was probably after his money," Chesna said. "You think that?"

"What other reason do certain women want to marry attractive men that dress nice?"

"I didn't really get that impression from her. She doesn't seem like the gold digger type."

"You know her?" Chesna asked. "No but I found out something about Vincent I don't like. He tried to make out with me in Vernon's house in the bathroom today."

"Does Vernon know?"

"No but I'm going tell him."

"You think that's a wise decision after what happened the last time?"

"I think it's better if I tell him than him finding out."

"You want me there with you when you tell him?"

"No. You don't have to be there."

"If he hits you I'm going to beat his ass."

"I'll be fine."

"If you say so."

"Just enjoy your birthday."

It was after eleven at night. Almost everyone left, except Glenda and Teely stuck around to help Vernon clean up. Vincent didn't do nothing but lean on the kitchen counter drinking his third beer for the night. Then he went to go sit on the living room couch. Vernon came through the living room with the trash bag full of trash. "Need some help?" Vincent asked. "No, I got it."

"I need to tell you something," Vincent said. "Come with me," Vernon said. They went outside. When Vernon sat the trash down, Vincent began to say," your lady is trying to come after me."

Vernon just looked at him. "Is she?" Vernon walked away. "I'm trying to let you know something."

"Yeah, I know," Vernon said but kept walking. Amber came back to Vernon's house at 1:30 in the morning. Her and the others went out to a club for a little while after Chesna's birthday dinner at Red Lobster. All the lights were out like how they sometimes were. Amber took off her high heel shoes because of her feet being sore from dancing in them. She turned on a lamp. Then Vernon appeared. "You have a good time?" he asked.

"Yeah, I need to tell you something."

He turned off the lamp. "Ready for bed?"

"Vernon listen your brother was trying to come at me here in your house."

They both stood there in the darkness with the streetlights bringing in some light through the window. Vernon loved how her lipstick gleamed in the moonlight. "You believe me, don't you?"

"Of course." He touched her face. "Let's get some sleep."

Amber turned over in bed and Vernon wasn't there. It was 9:45 Sunday morning. She had such great sleep she didn't want to get out of bed. Vernon came back and asked, "you up yet? Breakfast is ready."

Amber was eating up her waffles, bacon and hash browns while Vernon was cooking up more waffles. "How is it?" he asked. "Good. I wonder about you Vernon."

"Why?"

"Because you're doing things for me that you haven't done before."

"Maybe I'm trying to be the person I should have been before."

"I would never do you wrong. I want you to know that," Amber said. "I believe you. I told you before."

"Okay," she said, "I believe you."

Vernon phoned his brother to come over. Vernon was sitting at the kitchen table drinking his favorite cup of coffee. "Have a seat."

Vincent sits down. "This must be important for you to not want to talk over the phone."

"Let me start off by saying I don't know what you're trying to do, but I want you to leave my lady alone."

"Say what? I told you she tried to mess with me."

"I know you Vincent. You're a manipulator, a devil in disguise, and a back stabber."

"I'm your brother and you're talking to me like that."

"Well I've talked to your ex-fiancée Miranda. Oh yes, I sure did. She told me about your behavior while you two were together. She caught you in bed with some woman you work with and should I remind you you tried to sleep with my ex-wife ten years ago. Good looks and having a lot of money ain't everything."

Vincent folded his arms and leaned back in his chair. "I took you in, in spite of the things you have done and then you try to make a move on my woman in my house and to think mama thinks you're the better son. I don't want you over here anymore and you'd better stay away from Amber."

Vincent doesn't say a thing. He just left. Amber went to Chesna's place an hour after she left Vernon. "Did you tell Vernon about Vincent?"

"I did. His reaction was something that I didn't expect. He was calm about it."

"He probably already knew," Chesna said. "Maybe. Vernon's not the one you can get away with something. He did say he believes me."

"My prayers might have been answered," Chesna said. "What have you prayed about?"

"I prayed for both of you. I prayed he'd be a changed man since you were getting back with him. I want you to be happy."

"So do I," Amber said Glenda called Vernon on Vincent's phone at his house. "What's going on with you and Vincent?"

"What do you mean?"

"Vincent said you yelled at him this morning."

"I didn't yell at him. I just told him to leave my lady alone."

"You know your brother would do no such thing." "You apologize to my baby."

"Apologize! Look I'm not going to get into this with you mama. You, daddy, Teely and everybody else have a safe drive back to Kansas City good-bye!" Glenda stared at the receiver in her hand, hearing the dial tone. "What did he say mama?" Vincent asked. She just stood with her mouth open with the receiver still in her hand. Amber left her job at five, Monday evening. She rushed home just to relax. She threw her purse on the bed, then headed to the kitchen.

She discovered something in her kitchen she wasn't expecting to see. "Welcome home my lovely," Vincent said. "What are you doing here?"

"I wanted to see you and apologize for what happened over the weekend."

"Forgiven now can you leave?"

"I want to talk."

"I want you out or I'll call the police."

"You're not going to do that."

Amber went to the phone in the living room. When she picked up the phone, she didn't hear anything. She saw that her phone line was cut. "I had to do that, so we couldn't have any interruptions."

Vincent noticed she was looking at the front door. "What are you going to try to run?" He went to the front door to make sure it was locked. "You're not going anywhere."

"What do you want?"

"I want you and I want you to have me."

"I'm with Vernon."

"You I could have something going on."

"I am happy with the way my life is."

"You wouldn't have the life you have now if it wasn't for me. You would have been a miserable housewife changing diapers and wiping snotty noses by now."

"So what," Amber said. "So you owe," he said. Someone was knocking on the front door. Vincent pulled a thirty- eight from under shirt. "Don't say nothing," he said. Amber kept quiet like she told. She knew it had to be Chesna. She's the only person that really comes by, but Amber didn't understand what he had a gun for. Has he gone mad! Chesna knocked a few more times then left. Vincent then said. "We're going to your bedroom."

"What are we going in there for?" Vincent pointed the gun at her with a do what I told you look. They went to the bedroom. He shut the door. Amber stood still. Vincent went around behind her. He pressed the gun against her back. "Take off your clothes."

Chesna couldn't go anywhere but to Vernon. She went to his shop, but his employees said he left early. "Please be at home," she said to herself as she was driving. She was thanking God when she saw his Lexus in the driveway. Vernon was eating a bologna cheese sandwich when he opened the door. "Vernon, I need your help! Something's going on with Amber. I can't talk to her on the phone and she's not answering her door."

"Well we better get over there," Vernon said. He went back inside and came back out. "You'll have to show me where she lives because Amber didn't ever let me come visit her."

They were about to get in Vernon's car, but he noticed his front right tire was flat. Vernon took a close look at it. It looked like it was cut with a knife. How did this happen? He asked himself. He had an idea who and how, but he wanted to find out. "Let's talk," Amber said. "I don't want to talk, I want to have sex," Vincent said. "I thought you were a nice guy."

"You need to take off your clothes."

"If I don't then what? You're going to shoot me or rape me? You should think about this. The neighbors are going to hear the gun shots. You'll get put away for a long time. I don't know what's going on in your head but if shooting me is something you got to do---do it! I don't see what's it going to prove."

They heard a loud knock on the front door. Amber didn't look back. She left out of her bedroom not caring what he was going to do. No one wasn't going to keep her prisoner in her home. She opened her front door. "Thank goodness you're okay," Chesna said. "Is my brother here?" Vernon asked. "He certainly is."

"Vincent, where are you?" Vernon comes in looking around for his brother. Vincent crept out the bedroom. "What are you doing here?" Vernon asked. "I thought I told you to stay away from Amber!"

"You can't tell me what to do."

"It was you who cut my tire was it?"

"My own brother tells me not come around anymore. How do you think I should react to that?"

"Flattening my tire isn't the answer. What was you doing in the bedroom anyway?"

"Something I'm going to do to you." Vincent pulled out the thirty-eight on Vernon. "You really gone crazy," Vernon said. "I'm crazy. You shot yourself before."

"So now you think you can? You're not really a bright person. You put yourself in a position with no way out of it."

"I can shoot all of you and be gone before the police get here. That was my plan anyway."

"I hope you don't think you're going to get far?"

"I'm getting out of this state even this country with all the cash I got put away."

A loud and heavy knock was at the door. Vincent froze up. "Who could that be? Tell them to go away!" Amber got close to the door. "Who is it?" she asked. "Police!" they answered. "The police," Vincent said. "Yeah, I called the police after I left here earlier because

I was suspicious when I wasn't getting a response from Amber," Chesna said. "Jail time could do you some good, because when Mama finds out about this you'll rather be behind bars."

"Damn it! I should of just left town and said screw all of you," Vincent said. The police came in and arrested Vincent and took him away. Two months later, Amber celebrated her thirtieth birthday. She spent most of the day celebrating it with her friends but spent the evening with Vernon. He bought her a huge birthday cake. Neapolitan, her favorite. They ate much of it as they could with some champagne. Then they decided to burn off some of the calories by having sex. After, they just laid there in bed. "I wonder how my brother's doing."

"Oh, you worried about your little brother?" Amber asked. "Not really. He's a big boy. He can take care of himself. Your birthday's almost over and I almost forgot to give you your present." Vernon reached into a drawer next to the bed. He had a tiny box in his hand. "What's this?"

"Your engagement ring."

She opened the box. "It's the same ring," she said. "Yeah I kept it for you. I knew, or I hoped we end up back together. You want to try this again? I promise you things will be different."

"Yes, I really want to," Amber said. Vincent was sitting on the top bunk with his head down when the prison guard opened his cell and told him he had a visitor. When he went to the booth and saw Glenda, he panicked. "Mama!"

"Vincent! I'm gonna whoop your ass!" She broke the glass and grabbed him by the collar. Then she jumped on him and was choking him. "Help me! She's choking me, she's choking me!"

"Will you knock it off!" Vincent realized he was still in his cell and no one was choking him. "I'm sick of you and your damn nightmares," the skin head on the bottom bunk screamed. Vincent thought, *I'd rather be dead than see the day I get released from here.* Vernon and Amber got married in a downtown courthouse, the beginning of the new year. Chesna and Trent were the witnesses. They didn't tell either side of their families about the marriage, not even about the honeymoon. You, Me, He, and She

You, Me, He, and She

Spencer Taylor returns home to Baton Rouge, Louisiana, from Miami, Florida, about 2:00 a.m. His childhood friends, JD and Willy were at the airport waiting on him. JD gives him a hug and so does Willy. "Everything good?" JD asked. "Yes, Tye is doing good," Spencer answered. "How about up here? Everything alright at the crib?"

"Yep. You know LaTrish always holds it down."

"Speaking of crib, that's exactly where I'm going to get me some sleep."

"I was hoping you was coming by my place to play some pool, like we always do," Willy said. "Later. All I could think about on the plane was my bed. I'll come by when I get up."

"Cool what time will that be?"

"Probably about one o' clock this afternoon."

"Bet," Willy said. "Let's roll," JD said. Two forty-five in the morning, Spencer drops his luggage on the on floor as soon as he walks into his fancy house. The house was dark and quiet, but the kitchen light was on. He smelled seafood gumbo aroma in the air. Spencer goes to the kitchen; and his girlfriend, Latrish was in the kitchen. "LaTrish, what are you doing cooking at almost three 'o clock in the morning?"

"I got hungry."

"Couldn't you have just made a sandwich or something?"

"I missed you too Spence. I won't make a mess in your so extra clean kitchen."

LaTrish didn't say nothing else. She poured herself some gumbo in a bowl, then she searched for a spoon in one of the drawers. Spencer realized he up setted her. "Trish, I'm sorry baby. I didn't mean to be like that," he said, massaging her shoulders. "It's okay.

You're tired, and I'm tired. I'm going to watch some TV before I go to bed."

"Well I'm crashing, so goodnight," Spencer said. Spencer and JD went over to Willy's house to play some pool in his basement. All they did while playing pool was drink Colt 45's and talk a lot. Then Spencer got a call on his cell phone. "What's up?" he asked. "How come you didn't call me when you got back in town?" a woman named Ivori asked. "I was. I just now got back."

"So, when are you coming by to see me?" Ivori asked. "I don't know, later."

"You don't know! Well you need to know. I don't have all day."

"You know I'm a busy man."

"You're too busy for me?"

"I'll be by there later."

"Don't have me waiting all day."

Spencer hangs up. "That Ivori is something else."

"Yeah, she's fine as hell," JD said. "She don't know when to give somebody a break."

"That's why I'm not in a relationship," Willy said. "I'm not in a relationship with Ivori. She's just someone I screw. LaTrish is my baby."

"Then why are you cheating on her?" Willy asked. "I don't know. Maybe I'm just whipped."

Spencer showed up at Ivori's place until eleven that Saturday night. "It's about time you showed up," she said.

"Girl be quiet and fix me a glass of water. She got a pitcher of water out of the refrigerator and poured some water into a glass. "Thank you," he said, when she handed him the water. "You have some incents burning?"

"What you think?"

"It smells like something died."

"You smart ass."

Ivori starts taking Spencer's jacket off of him. "So, when are you going to stop playing ping-pong?" she asked. "Ping-pong?"

"Yes get rid of that little girl you got and just be with me. "I'll never do that."

Ivori folded her arms. "How come?"

"Because I'm just not."

"Don't I give you all the sexual pleasure in the world?"

"Is sex all you think about?" Spencer asked? "Is sex all you think about?" Ivori asked, with a mean look on her face. "You always like to argue with me, don't you?" Ivori was still looking at him with the mean look. "Be a good girl and cook me something to eat."

Spencer tip-toed up the stairs to his bedroom at three fifteen Sunday morning. He undressed and jumped in the shower. LaTrish wasn't all the way asleep. Ten minutes later, Spencer finished his shower, dried off, put on his boxers and climbed in bed next to LaTrish, dosing off. LaTrish was faced away from him. Then she sat up in bed, looking at Spencer. Spencer, we need to talk."

"Talk about what?" he asked, with his eyes closed. "Where have you've been all night?"

"Can we talk about this later?" He rolls over and goes to sleep. "Spencer! Spence! Spencer was knocked out. LaTrish came home from church that afternoon. Spencer was eating a pear ready to head out the door. "Spencer where are you going? We need to talk."

"I don't have time to talk. I have runs to make."

That's it, shut the door and leave with no hello or good-bye kisses. "I guess I'm the invisible woman," she said. LaTrish goes upstairs to the bedroom to change out of her church clothes in this big empty house, again. LaTrish worked days through the week at a clinic. Spencer was an assistant manager at a warehouse plant that assembled toys and he was also selling drugs on the side with his cousin, Tye who was in a wheelchair since he was nineteen. He had an accident on a construction site. Tye and Spencer had been close since their childhood. That's why he's always back and forth from Baton Rouge to Miami. LaTrish spent every night through the week alone in her bed. One Thursday night it rained so hard, it scared her. Seeing a lightening bolt touch the ground made her grab hold of her pillow. She wished Spencer was here to comfort her like he used to Saturday was the day LaTrish had her French classes. LaTrish eats at this café after every class. A guy approached her table. "You mind if I sit with you?"

"She stared at him."

"I'm Mardy Cleaton."

"Yes, you're in my French class. I didn't recognize you without your glasses," LaTrish said. Mardy stared at her. "I'm sorry please sit down."

He sat across from her. "So, do you enjoy learning French?" he asked. "Yeah, I plan on learning German also so whenever I get to go to France or Germany, I'll know how to speak it."

"Cool. I'm just taking up French because I failed it in high school."

"You seem like a smart guy."

"I am. But I'm glad I failed French in high school because I wouldn't be here looking at a beautiful woman and I know I'm going to ace this class because there's some things I would love to say to you in French."

LaTrish was blushing. "What are you doing tonight," Mardy asked. "Are you trying to ask me out?"

"Yes."

"I'm sorry I do have a boyfriend."

"Oh, my bad. I should of known. I bet your man takes you out every weekend."

LaTrish shook her head. "He seems to be busy all the time."

"He should have some kind of time for you."

"Nope he doesn't."

"What good is a relationship if there's no quality time."

"Tell that to him," she said. "Why are you with him?"

"I guess I love him. He does keep a roof over my head."

"It seems he doesn't spend time with you because he's spending it with someone else. I'm willing to give you the quality time you deserve. Starting right now. I'm not trying to get you to cheat on your man…I want to show you what a real man can do."

"You saying my man ain't a real man?"

"He's doing his job of keeping you happy. I can make you happy. Let me show you and you'll see."

Spencer was over at Ivori's in her bedroom, giving it to her doggie style. After they were finished, Spencer showered and got dressed. "Where are you heading to now?" Ivori asked. "Just some important runs I got to make" he answered, "I didn't realize how late in the day it was."

"You always want to do a hit and run," she said. "Well you always seem to like it like that. Someone was knocking on the door. Ivori put on her bathrobe and they both went in the living room. "Who you got coming over?" Spencer asked. Ivori rushed to the door. She let a man with a little boy, in. The man handed her a book bag. She didn't introduce neither to each other. The man didn't pay Spencer no attention anyway. After the man left, Ivori took her son to his room. Spencer was standing in the living room waiting for her to explain what was going on. She came back in the living room, looking at the expression on Spencer's face. "What was that?"

"My baby's daddy. Please don't ask me any more questions. I'm going to spend some time with my son."

Spencer leaves. While driving down the road, he dials up LaTrish. Her phone continued to ring. That was a first. LaTrish have always answered her phone. He dialed her again. Then her phone said, "No one is able to take your call, please try again later."

When Mardy and LaTrish left the café, they walked and talked in the park. Then they went bowling. Then that evening they went to the movies. They drank sodas, ate nachos, laughed, having a good time. Spencer was at home wondering where could LaTrish be. She was always at home. He was worried but also a little mad. After the movies, Mardy and LaTrish was in the parking lot standing by LaTrish's car. "I haven't had so much fun like this in a long time," she said. "I had fun too," he said. "I hope your man won't be mad at me for taking you out."

"He's too busy to notice."

Spencer had left the house and went by JD's place for a moment. He came back home by eleven that night and parked his car in the garage. Spencer tried calling LaTrish again but still he didn't get in touch with her. Spencer was standing in the refrigerator, drinking a cold glass of water when he heard the front door open. He startled LaTrish when she came into the kitchen. "Spence, I didn't know you were here."

"My car is in the garage. What's up with you? Why haven't you been returning my phone calls?"

"You've never called or worried about me before."

Spencer slammed the refrigerator door shut. He was completely butt naked. "How come you don't have any clothes on?"

"It's my house. I can walk around in it however I want." He came closer to her. "Why haven't you been answering my phone calls?"

"I've told you already."

Spencer squinted his eyes at her. "I've been busy."

"What, getting busy with another man?" LaTrish got upset. "I'm going to bed," she said. "I'm not done talking to you yet."

"What is it Spencer? Are you going to hit me?" Spencer stared at her hard then he just went upstairs. LaTrish went right to sleep as Spencer laid beside her, watching her sleep, trying to figure out who this man is. He was afraid of losing her to someone else but him cheating on her for the longest, was beginning to make Spencer feel bad Spencer had gotten up early Sunday morning because he didn't get much sleep last night. He, JD, and Willy went out to eat breakfast. Then they came back to Spencer's place. JD and willy wanted in the living room while spencer went back to his car. LaTrish was coming down the stairs, dressed up. JD and Willy was eyeballing her. "Hello gentlemen."

"What's going on baby girl?" JD asked. "Oh,, nothing just on my way to church."

"Could we follow you because you're sure wearing the hell out of that dress," Willy said. Spencer came back in. "Where are you going?" he asked. "You know I'm going to church and maybe you should go to because Jesus can save you from your sins. See you later." LaTrish leaves. "You're lucky to have such a good woman. I'd wish I had a woman like that," JD said. Spencer said nothing. Spencer and Ivori were sitting up in her bed, smoking a joint and watching a movie on DVD. "Ivori go to the store for me."

"For what?"

"I want a six pack of Miller Light."

"I want to finish watching this movie."

"I'll pause it. Take the car and get me some Miller Light."

Ivori sighed. Spencer gave her the keys to his car and she left LaTrish went to the grocery store after church. She was in the produce section, getting some apples when a man came by. "Excuse me miss…do I know you?"

"Hello Mardy," she said. "How you doing LaTrish?"

"I'm good and you?"

"I'm great now that I've seen you. Grocery shopping?" he asked. "Yeah, I'm cooking today."

"Too bad you have a man because I would love to try your cooking… you still have a man, don't you?"

"Yes," she said, sadly. "If you're not happy LaTrish, you know what to do."

"Yeah," she said. "I would like to take you out again, but I don't want to interfere."

"I know," LaTrish said. "See you in French class," Mardy said. "See ya."

He left. LaTrish took her cell phone out of her purse and called Spencer. Spencer down in bed when she called. "Hi Spence, it's me."

"What's up?" Spencer asked. "I'm cooking today."

"Really what are you cooking?"

"Spaghetti with some garlic bread and maybe we can have some wine."

"That sounds good."

"So, when you coming home?"

"Soon," he answered. "Ok, bye," LaTrish said. Ivori arrived at the grocery store. She went straight to the liquor department. She got the Miller Light and went to check out. LaTrish got into the checkout line next to the one Ivori was in. Neither one knew about each other even though Ivori knew Spencer had a girlfriend living with him. LaTrish got through her line before Ivori did. LaTrish rolled her basket of groceries out to her car. While she was putting the groceries in her car, LaTrish happened to see Spencer's car in the parking lot. She didn't want to believe it, but she knew his license plate number. *Is he in the store?* She asked herself. Then she saw Ivori come out, get into his car and drive away in it. She just couldn't believe any of this. But at least she knows the truth now. At first, LaTrish thought Spencer had turned gay on her because of him not wanting to have sex with her or kiss her or even just touching her. LaTrish got in her car and called Spencer again. "Hello," Spencer said. "It's me again." She paused. "Is something wrong?" he asked. She still stayed quiet but then she said, "no nothing's wrong."

Then LaTrish hung up. "LaTrish…Hello…LaTrish!" Spencer hung up and tried to call her. She wouldn't answer her phone. Ivori came back to her place. Spencer was staring at his phone. "Got your six-pack."

He was still staring at his phone. "Who was you talking to?" Ivori asked. "Nobody," he answered Hours have passed. LaTrish was sitting in the kitchen drinking out of the wine bottle. She didn't even attempt to cook anything. LaTrish felt she shouldn't have to cook for someone who doesn't appreciate her. All she could picture was him making love to that woman while she's sitting here day after day wondering if he is ever going to come back. *What the hell does he expect me to do?* LaTrish asked herself, *go along with it? He got me messed up.* This my life. She drank the entire bottle of wine to the last drop. When she stood up, she felt tipsy. LaTrish threw the bottle in the trash and headed upstairs. She almost tripped on the stairs because the stairway looked as if it was moving. It took a moment for her to get to the top, but she made it. LaTrish fell into bed. She slept for an hour. Then she woke up, sweating. LaTrish ran for the shower and she cleansed herself thoroughly. She leaned against the tile wall, letting the warm water hit her skin and her breathing hard, thinking what if Spencer found her dead, like drowned herself. How would he act? *He probably wouldn't miss me. He acts like I don't even exist, sometimes. But what would killing myself prove? I don't want to burn in hell either.* She heard someone come in the bedroom. Then she heard footsteps coming toward the bathroom. LaTrish could see Spencer standing there through the shower curtain. He pulled back the shower curtain. Spencer stared at her and LaTrish stared back. Then she snatched the shower curtain back. Spencer pulled it back again and said, "what are you doing?"

"What does it look like I'm doing?"

"Why did you call and then wouldn't answer when I called you?"

"Why are you sleeping with another woman?"

"What?"

"Don't play with me Spencer. I damn well you're not hanging out with JD and Willy all the time."

"You're right, I don't."

"Why are you doing this to me? Oh, I get it, I don't have a fat ass like she does."

"That has nothing to do with it," Spencer said. "Then why?" LaTrish turns off the water and wraps herself in a towel. Spencer follows her in the bedroom. She sat on the bed. He stands with his hands in his pockets. "How come you're not saying nothing?" LaTrish asked. "What do you want me to say?" Spencer asked. "I guess you don't love me. It's her you love. I must gross you out, do I Spence?"

"How do you know what I think about you?" Spencer asked. "What the hell do you expect me to think? You don't want to talk to me. How do you expect me to feel? There's no communication here. Have you forgotten what planet this is?" Spencer was looking down at his feet, rubbing his nose. "Well I guess you don't care. Now neither do I." LaTrish went back into the bathroom and slammed the door.

He stands by the bathroom door listening to her cry her little heart out.

"LaTrish baby… I love you. I love everything about you. Even that body of yours."

"You're just telling me what I want to hear. You're not going to leave her."

"LaTrish!"

"Go away Spencer! Leave me alone! He left out of the house. LaTrish stayed locked in the bathroom, sitting on the floor, crying for hours LaTrish was sitting in the break room at her job slowly nibbling on her grilled chicken salad. "What's up, girly?" Jasaline Bates asked. Jasaline was Latrish's co-worker and JD's baby's mama. She sat down at the table, getting ready to grubb on some cooked catfish she bought at the fish market. Jasaline looked at LaTrish. "Why are you looking so depressed? I know it's Monday, but you've been looking like that all day."

"I'm just not feeling myself today."

"I understand girlfriend." Jasaline paused. "I know it's none of my business, but I heard about Spencer's other girl. I'm sorry LaTrish."

"It's alright."

"You love Spencer, don't you?"

"I love him a lot."

"If I were you, I wouldn't let any woman steal my man away from me. Especially a I can do for you that your girl can't do type of female. Because that's what she is. Somebody who has nothing to offer but their body. He ain't serious about her. You know what you should do… buy a bad ass outfit, get your hair and nails done. That will get you some attention from other guys and Spencer's attention away from miss nobody. He'll be worried some other guy will take you away from him. He'd better wake up. "Yeah, but Spencer is a nice guy. He's one man that is highly educated and holds a steady job," LaTrish said. "But when it comes to a woman's heart he's not taking that too seriously," Jasaline said. "Take control LaTrish, take control. Nothing has changed even since LaTrish found out about Spencer's mystery lady. Again, she has spent the whole week alone at night. LaTrish was sitting in front of her bedroom mirror on a Friday night, telling her reflection it's time to make that move. LaTrish was about to leave when Spencer came back home Saturday morning. "Leaving?" he asked. "Yes, I'm about to go to my French class…and I'm moving out."

"Why?"

"You know why. We've talked about this before."

"Come on LaTrish, she ain't nothing but some broad I met at some after party."

LaTrish just left Mardy kept staring at LaTrish in French class because of the expression on her face that shows she's going through something. They both went to the café after class. "I told him I'm moving out. I'm fed up with the lonely nights and feeling like I'm always alone."

"How did he react to it?" Mardy asked. "He tried to act like he wasn't mad but deep down I know Spencer doesn't damn. I have a cousin that is going to let me stay with her. I mean I can get a place of my own, I can't afford to be by myself. I need comfort I need to be around love what you really need is some spice in your life. How about we go out tonight?" he asked. "Where?"

"Dancing at a club…you have been to a club before?"

"Yes, it's been a while."

"We'll meet back here like…nine o' clock," Mardy said. "I'll be here," LaTrish said. LaTrish was standing in front of the bathroom mirror, combing her thinking about what Mardy asked, *you have been to a club before? Like I'm some nerd or something* She thought the same about him. *Dressing like a private school boy or looking like he's getting ready to play golf. He's a totally different man from Spencer.* LaTrish seen different when they met back up at the café. She was sitting in her favorite spot waiting on him. Here he came in from the pouring rain not wearing glasses, clean shaven and looking a lot more like a fashion model. "Sorry I'm late, time gotten away," he said. "That's okay I just got here myself."

"You're ready?" Mardy asked. "Yeah."

Before they walked out the door, LaTrish saw how heavy the rain was coming down. "Oh, no," she said. "What's wrong?"

"I didn't bring a jacket or an umbrella."

Mardy took off his expensive leather jacket and put it around her. "You alright now?' She nodded her head. They rode in Mardy's car to the club. Mardy was a real gentleman. He opened the car door for LaTrish, offered to pay her way in the club and offered to buy her a drink. Mardy had three drinks before they got out on the dance floor. LaTrish knew he had to be drunk because he kept cheesing and laughing when they were slow dancing, but he was still a gentleman. He held her close while she laid her head on his shoulder. "I never did tell you how nice you look tonight," Mardy said. LaTrish lifted her head and looked him in the eyes. He was still smiling. She smiled back. "I think you look nice too."

Mardy kissed her, lightly then he started tongue kissing her She pushed him away. "Mardy don't…it's too soon."

"I'm sorry, you want another drink?"

"No thanks."

"Well I'm getting another drink."

"Mardy I don't think you should drink anymore."

"Come on girl have some fun."

Mardy had two more drinks. He was for sure drunk. LaTrish took his keys from him so she could drive the both of them home. Her night was ruined LaTrish helped Mardy into his place. He staggered over to his couch and plopped right on it. She took her cell phone out of her purse. "What are you doing?" he asked. "I'm calling cab."

"Don't leave. Stay here tonight."

"I should get going."

Mardy tried to stand up but he went back down. "LaTrish baby the night is still young…don't leave me here by myself."

She sat on the edge of the couch. "Lay back," she said. Mardy laid back. "My cab is coming in few minutes. "I got some slow music we can dance to," Mardy said. "You can't even stand up."

"Yes, I can."

Mardy got up and tried to run to his room for a CD but he ran into the wall. He fell backwards on floor. LaTrish rushed over to him. "Mardy you okay?"

"Damn my head hurts!" he cried. She helped him to his bedroom. He laid down on his bed. "You should take a cold shower and get some rest," LaTrish said. Mardy gently touched her face. "LaTrish."

She touched his hand, the hand that was on her face. "I'll get back with you, my cab is probably outside."

Mardy was getting sleepy. In the next minute, he was snoring. LaTrish crept out of his room and then waited by the front of his house until her taxi came. LaTrish rode the taxi back to the café where she left her car. The rain had eased up a little. After she got into her car and started it up, her cell phone rang. She looked at it and saw Spencer's number. She ignored it. She didn't want to go back home because he might be there. To her surprise, he wasn't. LaTrish sat on the couch, took off her shoes, and propped her feet up on the table. She laid back to relax her mind and body. Her cell phone rung again. She ignored it. It rung again for a long time. She answered it. "Spencer, I don't feel like talking."

"LaTrish do you really want to move out?"

"Yes, I do."

"Where are you now?" Spencer asked. "That's not important good-bye."

She turned her phone off. Her mind was made up. Spencer and Ivori were sitting in the bed watching TV while Ivori's son was lying at the end of the bed coloring in his coloring book. Spencer was upset because LaTrish hung up on him. He got up and went to bathroom where he left his phone on the sink. He called her but couldn't get through. He threw his phone across the bathroom and it hit the wall. Spencer cussed because he thought he broke his phone. Luckily, he didn't. Ivori came running. "What's the matter with you?" she asked. Spencer pushed her out of the way. He put on his jacket and shoes, then headed for the door. Ivori jumped in front of him. "What is going on with you and who do you keep calling?"

"Don't worry about it."

She blocked the front door. "You're not leaving."

"Get the hell out of my way!"

"No!" she screamed. He pushed her out of his way then slammed the door behind him. Spencer went to his house. He saw that LaTrish had took all her clothes and personal things. Spencer knows now that he really messed up. LaTrish woke up stretching and yawning at her cousin Laci's house. She smelled the smell of Sunday morning breakfast her Aunt Bassie was cooking, oatmeal, toast and bacon. "Aunt Bassie, I knew it was you that was cooking up a storm."

"Hi sugar," Bassie said. They gave each other kisses on the cheek. "You going to eat some breakfast?"

"Yes, I'm hungry."

"I'm giving you extra because you look like you've lost a few pounds."

"I've been stressing."

"Your job?"

"No other things."

"That's not healthy. Don't let life put you under stress."

Bassie sat LaTrish's plate on the table. Laci's two kids Neena and Tyree came running in the kitchen. "Stop running in the house!" Bassie said. "Hi Trissie," Neena and Tyree said. "Hi," LaTrish said back. "Sit down and eat," Bassie, told her grandkids. They both sat down while Bassie poured everybody a glass of orange juice. "Grandma can we get twenty dollars, so we can go to the mall today?" Neena asked. "Why don't you ask your mama?"

"We did. She told us to ask you."

"What's Laci doing anyway?" LaTrish asked, while eating her oatmeal. "Getting ready for church," Bassie answered. LaTrish stood up. "I need to talk to her. "Sit your butt back down and finish your breakfast."

"Yes ma'am." LaTrish sat down and finished her breakfast. Laci was standing in front of her bedroom mirror, curling her hair with the curling iron. "Going to church today, huh?" LaTrish asked. "Yep, trying to keep the spirit," Laci said. "So how you feeling?"

"Okay I guess."

"So, what's the scoop on you and Spencer?"

"He's not feeling me. He has another woman he thinks is better than me."

"Better than you?"

"She must have something that I don't have."

"She ain't got nothing different from any other woman. She probably told him that she can do for him that no other woman can do. Dumb men listen to that stuff. They don't use the head on their shoulders. They listen to what's in their pants. "You know out of all the guys, I thought he was the one. Now it's going to be hard for me to believe that any man is going to take me seriously."

"It's not the end of the world," Laci said, "that's what I've been telling myself ever since that pathetic ex-husband and I split up. I've been praying everyday to God to bless me with a good man." Laci combs her hair in place and takes a look at it. Then she looks at LaTrish. "The right man will come at the right time."

LaTrish agreed by slowly nodding her head. Mardy followed LaTrish out to her car after class. "I'm sorry for how I acted last weekend. I came on too strong and I don't want you to be afraid of me. I do want to take you out again."

"I don't know Mardy. I just got out of a relationship. I need to think about it."

"Yeah, think about it. I'll treat you right." He rubs her hand.

Spencer was sitting in her car watching them, with Willy and JD. "I knew she had someone else," Willy said. "Yeah, she's been looking hot lately," JD said. Spencer was just staring at Mardy thinking, *that's what she wants? That's what she wants over me?* Spencer gets out of the car and walks over to them. "I hope he's not going to do nothing crazy," Willy said. "LaTrish!" Spencer said. Mardy and LaTrish looked. "What are you doing here?' LaTrish asked. "I wanna talk to you."

"Why? You never had time before."

"I'm here now."

"Well talk."

Spencer looked at Mardy. "He's going to have to step."

Mardy got mad. "Look partner, you going to have to leave," Spencer said. "LaTrish do you want me to leave?" Mardy asked. "We're just going to talk right quick. I'll come by and see you," LaTrish said. Mardy got in his car and took off. "Who do you think you are Spencer?"

"I'm your man ain't I?"

"No, you can't have me and somebody else."

"She's nobody. When have I brought another woman in our house… in our bed?"

"I don't know, have you?"

"How long you've been boning him?"

"I'm not even sleeping with him but if I was it wouldn't be none of your business."

"I let you stay in a big beautiful house. There's a lot of women that would love to be where you are."

"Don't be trying to make it look like I'm materialistic. I have my own job my own money and I had my own place when I met you. I only agreed to live with you because I thought we was in love, eventually get married. But it's all making sense now. All you wanted was a good woman you can come home to, so you can be out with these skanks!"

"LaTrish "No Spencer. It's best that we stay out of each other's way. You're making it obvious that you're not going to stop doing what you are doing. I'll give you back the key when I get the rest of my things."

LaTrish got away from Spencer to catch up with Mardy. She hoped he was at home. They sat down on the couch after Mardy let her in. "Now I'll have to apologize to you LaTrish said. "Don't worry about it," he said. "Really all we should be is friends, only seeing each other in French class."

Mardy was disappointed. "LaTrish all I wanna be is that man that wants to do everything that you want to do."

"I really don't know much about you," she said. "I'm a lonely man. I haven't had a girlfriend in six months. I took culinary arts straight out of high school. That's why I'm a chef that works in a big fancy restaurant. I'm Baptist, the only child…anything else you want to know?"

"No that's fine for now."

"I've always had my eyes on you no matter how many women I pass by in the streets, you're the one girl I dream about in my sleep and I'm not just saying that."

"That's sweet. I think you're a nice looking man, but I think it's best we don't see each other, at least not right now."

He sighed. "I guess I have to go along with that." He walked her to the door. "I'll see you," she said. They stared at each other. Mardy wanted to kiss her but he held back. He watched her get in her car and drive down the road until he couldn't see the car no more. All work and no play, that's all LaTrish did was work the whole week but at night she'll be lying in her bed thinking about Mardy. She tried not to. But she was glad to be over Spencer. LaTrish wasn't worried about him one bit. LaTrish went to her French class on Saturday but Mardy wasn't there. The next Saturday, which was the final day of the six - month course, Mardy still didn't show. She was hoping that he wasn't upset with her because of Spencer. *Damn he's going to flunk French again,* LaTrish thought to herself Spencer could barely concentrate at his job and he couldn't think straight at home since LaTrish told him they were through. He couldn't call her anymore because she changed her number. He couldn't even think about trying to see her because Laci would whoop his ass. A call came through on his phone. He didn't look to see who it was, he just answered it. "Where are you?" Ivori asked. Spencer sighed. "I'm at home."

"Well come pick me up."

"For what?"

"Because I need to go somewhere."

"Did I leave a jacket over there?"

"The brown leather one?" Ivori asked. "Yes," he answered. "Yeah, you did. Hey, are you going to come get me or what?"

"I'll be over there."

"Come in," Ivori said, when Spencer arrived. His jacket was laying on the couch and he grabbed it. Ivori had her purse. "Ready when you are."

"What are you doing?" Spencer asked. "Aren't you taking me shopping?"

"No, I never said I was."

"What?"

"Why don't you catch the bus or have that baby daddy of yours drive you. I know you've been having him over here."

"So, what does that have anything to do with you?"

"Nothing."

"Who the hell are you? I can have whoever I want in here because it's my house. I pay the bills in here. "Woman you don't pay nothing. Us taxpayers pay for you to have a roof over your head and watch soap operas five days a week."

"I hate you," Ivori said. Someone was calling Spencer on his phone. He went to the bathroom to talk. Spencer left both sets of keys laying on top of the jacket he left there. Spencer came back from the bathroom. "I gotta roll, I gotta leave town tomorrow evening." He grabbed his keys and jacket.

After he left, Ivori had a satisfying look on her face.

LaTrish went to Mardy's house after she left from work. She knocked several times, but he didn't answer. LaTrish knew he had to be there because his car was in the driveway. So she decided to forget about it.

Spencer was packing his clothes for his flight to Miami tomorrow. He picked up both sets of keys that were lying on the bed because he was on his way out to his car. He noticed one of his house keys were missing. He knew it was on the key ring before he went to Ivori's house. So Spencer called over there to see if she has seen a key lying around. She told him she did find a key. He hurried over to get it. Spencer didn't thank her or show any gratitude when she gave him the key because he knew in the back of his mind that she took that key. It was three hours ago when she took that key. Enough time to go make a copy. Ivori knew he was going to be back for it, but she didn't think this soon because it was just an extra spare key. So when Spencer was on his way over, she called Brownie, a crackhead who drove a raggedy Buick to follow Spencer and find out where he lived. She offered him twenty dollars for doing it. Brownie followed him and came back with an address. Ivori got what she wanted, and Brownie got what he wanted.

Laci and LaTrish were getting ready to go out to the club on a Saturday night.

"Should I wear these earrings or these earrings?" Laci asked LaTrish.

LaTrish didn't say anything. She was sitting in front of the mirror, brushing her hair.

"LaTrish!"

"Yes!"

"Are you listening to me girl?"

"Yes."

"You still thinking about that meathead Spencer?"

"No."

"How come you've been brushing that same spot on your head for the last twenty minutes?"

"I don't really want to go out."

"LaTrish, you need to go out and live your life. Have some fun, meet people."

"A club is not the place to meet no man. You should know that, miss suppose-to-be churchgoing woman."

"Okay, your choice," Laci said.

LaTrish stayed at the house while Laci went out and her kids stayed over with Bassie. She wanted some peace. Some peace of mind. But for some reason Mardy kept crossing her mind. She didn't want to think about him but couldn't help it. LaTrish got in her car and drove to his house.

Why am I here? she asked herself when she parked in front of his house. *He's here but he might not answer like the last time.* LaTrish decided to try again. She rang the doorbell, waited patiently for a second, but then decided to leave. As she headed back to her car, Mardy came to the door and called her name.

"Oh, Mardy," she said with a smile as she turned around.

"I'm surprised to see you," Mardy said.

"I know this is an odd time to be stopping by, but I was just wondering about you because I haven't seen you in a while."

"I had to leave town because my grandmother ended up in the hospital."

"Is she all right?"

"She's fine now. She's at home. Right now, I'm just getting off work, getting ready to get in the shower."

"Oh, don't let me interrupt you. I just wanted to say hello."

"Well, since you're here…you want to come in? I brought some food from work you might like."

"Okay," she said. She followed him through his living room into his dining room.

"Have a seat," he said.

LaTrish sat down.

Mardy went into the kitchen and got a plate. He took out a to-go box out of a plastic bag that was sitting on the table in front of her.

"That smells good… what is it?"

"Shrimp scampi. I made it myself."

He handed her a plastic fork. "Help yourself. I'm going to take my shower." He leaves her to eat.

While she's eating, LaTrish thinks, *what's going to happen next?* Mardy was in the shower thinking, *I really like this woman, and hope she'll spend the night. But she did say she just wants to be just friends. Then again, why would she be here this late?* Mardy was imaging him and her taking a shower together, close, cleansing each other. When he finished his shower, Mardy went straight to the kitchen, into the refrigerator and sat a bottle of peach champagne with two tall glasses in front of LaTrish. She didn't say nothing but, "that was delicious."

"Something to drink?" he asked. "No thank you. I don't want to drive home drunk."

"I was hoping you'd stay."

"Mardy, I…I promise I won't get drunk and silly on you," he said. "Well we're not actually ahhh…boyfriend and girlfriend," Mardy finished for her. "Yeah."

"We can be. That's if you wanna try to be more than friends," he said. LaTrish wouldn't say anything. She wouldn't even look at him. She was looking down at her hands. LaTrish continued to stare at her hands. Mardy was looking confused. Then LaTrish looked at him. She stands up and kisses him. After the kiss she gazes into his eyes and says, "I want to be more than friends but tonight just isn't the night."

He followed her to the front door desperately wanting to keep her here, but he let her leave She didn't look back. Ivori haven't been able to make it over to Spencer's house because she had to keep her son all week, all day, each day. When Sunday came, her son was able to be with his father and grandmother in church. So today was the day. Ivori got on the city bus, heading for Spencer's place. After she got on the bus she thought, *oh snap, what if he came back from Miami already? On the hand, he might be still gone, because Spencer likes to spend time in Miami. Not just because of his cousin but all the hot women down there.* She was afraid of his reaction if she showed up at his doorstep. When Ivori got to her destination, she had to walk a block to his house. It looked like no one was home. She slowly eased her way to the front door. Ivori took the key out of her pants pocket and put it in the lock, hoping this the right house and nobody was watching. Her heart began to beat fast when the door unlocked. At last she finally entering the doorway of this secret place. Ivori couldn't believe how huge and gorgeous it was. She shut the door as soon as she got in. The living room was so neat. Not a crumb on the floor. It smelled so good too. She noticed this house had an upstairs, so she went upstairs. Ivori knew the bedrooms had to be up there, but she wondered how many were there? She turned left down the hallway to a closed door, but it was locked. Then she went the other way down the hall and there was a door halfway opened. Ivori crept into the room. It was a big master bedroom. Ivori couldn't help looking at the king-sized bed with the expensive comforter and sheets. She hurried

and happily jumped on the bed. She was laying down saying, "I've always wondered how it felt to make love in an expensive bed. Ivori stopped that thought right there and sat up. "Spencer probably have been screwing that girl in this bed many times. Ivori looked around the room. She went over to the bathroom and turned on the light. She was loving it. How decorated it was. Ivori started playing with her hair in the mirror. Then she heard a woman's voice calling Spencer's name from downstairs. "Damn," Ivori said. She stayed in the bathroom peeking out. Ivori heard the woman call Spencer's name again and heard footsteps coming up the stairs. LaTrish came into the room and threw her purse on the bed. "The girlfriend," ivory said to herself. LaTrish went to the closet and grabbed a box of shoes she left, off the shelf. LaTrish had her back to Ivori. She stared at her hard from behind the bathroom door. What the hell does Spencer see in this scrawny little girl? LaTrish turns around to pick up her purse, she sees Ivori standing on the other side of bed. LaTrish was in deep shock. "Well, so you're the one. Spencer's secret girlfriend and secret home that he's been trying to keep from me. You think you're number one…
not anymore."

"You get out of here!" LaTrish said. Ivori went toward LaTrish. "You might as well give Spencer up. He's never gonna be just yours."

"Get the hell out of my way!" LaTrish said. LaTrish heads out of the room to the stairs. Something flared up in Ivori, so she went after her. "Why don't you disappear," Ivori cried when she came behind LaTrish and pushed her. She went tumbling down the stairs with her purse and box of shoes. It was a long flight of stairs that and LaTrish didn't move when she landed on the floor. Ivori ran down the stairs. She looked at LaTrish. She still wasn't moving. Ivori realized she did something terrible so she ran out the house. LaTrish woke up forty-five minutes later, with her left forearm broken, her lower right side scraped up and a bump on her head that made the room spin. She tried to move, but, couldn't. LaTrish hoped that Spencer would return soon. Her head was starting to hurt. Then she went unconscious. Shortly after, JD stopped by to check on Spencer's place. "What the…," he said when he saw Latrish lying on the floor. "LaTrish you alright?" He tried to wake her, but she wouldn't move. JD went to the kitchen where the phone was on the bar. "Hey Willy, have you gotten to the airport yet?"

"Not yet," Willy said. "I'm here at Spencer's house and I found Latrish lying unconscious on the floor."

"Damn," Willy said. "I'm gonna call the paramedics."

"I'll let Spencer know as soon as I see him."

"Later," JD said. Spencer and Willy got to the hospital as soon as they could. Spencer asked the lady at the front desk what room was LaTrish Grand was in. She told them what room. JD was in the hallway when they got there. "How is she?" Spencer asked. "The doctor said she fractured her arm and a few scrapes but she'll be okay."

Spencer went in the room. LaTrish had her eyes closed. He touched her gently on the face."

"LaTrish."

She opened her eyes. "LaTrish baby, what happened?" She leaned forward and smacked the mess out of him. "I went by your house to get some shoes I left, and that woman was there."

"Was she trying to steal?"

"I don't know what she was doing. She sort, of, snuck up on me. Then she started talking stuff. When I was trying to leave, she came up behind me and next thing I knew, I was going down the stairs."

"I'm sorry that this happened. She shouldn't have been there."

When Spencer left the hospital, he went straight to Ivori's place. She was sunk down in the living room chair with her robe on, smoking some weed. She began shaking with fear when she heard the heavy knock on the door. Ivori hopped up out of the chair, shaking even more when the knocking continued. "Ivori are you in there?"

"Spencer!" she said. "Yeah," he answered. Ivori stood by the door but didn't answer it. "What did you need?" she asked. "I want to see you. I just got back in town and while I was gone I've been thinking about us…how everything went down before I left. I was just in one of those moods."

Ivori loved the sound of his voice when he apologizes, and it was so sincere. "If you let me in, I'll make it up to you."

She slowly reaches for the door knob. Then she slowly unlocks the door. Spencer pushes the door open. "Where's that freakin' key at and what was you doing in my house?"

"Nothing."

"Oh, nothing. You were doing something. I know about what happened over there earlier. You could get in a lot of trouble for that."
"But she attacked me. Her clumsy ass fell down those steps on her own." "I'm sorry. What can I do for you not to be upset with me."

"You know what you got to do," Spencer said. Ivori got on her knees, while Spencer was still standing. Then she started unzipping his pants. Bassie and Laci stopped at the hospital later that day. "Girl what happened to you?" Laci asked. "I know it has something to do with Spencer. He's beating on you, isn't he?"

"No Laci he's not," LaTrish said. "How did this happen then?" Bassie asked. "I just had an accident."

"You couldn't have gotten hurt this badly by missing a few steps," Bassie said. LaTrish wouldn't say anything else. "What's going on with you?" her Aunt asked. "Mama it's Spencer she's trying to protect. Don't let me run into him, I'll bust him in the mouth. There's also some stuff I found out about him."

"What's that?" LaTrish asked. "He's a drug dealer. He's using that job he has to cover it up."

"You sure you got the right person."

"Yes, Jasaline told me at church."

"Did you know this?" Bassie asked LaTrish. "Course not."

"If you're broken up with Spencer like you say you are, I'm glad because no telling what could of happened to you if he got caught. But he's going to get caught one day. "You want something to eat?" Bassie asked. "Some Popeye's chicken."

"Okay we'll back in a little bit," Laci said. Bassie and Laci brought back some Popeye's chicken. They stayed for a moment then they left. The day was going by. LaTrish wondered if Spencer coming back. He hasn't been back since morning. There was one face she didn't expect to see. "Mardy I'm surprised to see you."

"I'm glad to see you but not in a hospital bed. I called over to your cousin's house for you. She told me you were in the hospital, sick. So, I rushed over here. I was hoping it wasn't because of some food that was bad that I gave to you. I can see it wasn't. He was looking at the sling her arm was in. "May I ask what happened?" LaTrish wouldn't tell him. Mardy looked at her like he knows. "It's not Spencer," she said. "I fell down the stairs."

"Please don't use that with me. You battered women are always trying to protect these crazy men."

"Battered women! Who the hell are you to be judging somebody?"

"I'm sorry, I didn't mean to make you upset."

"I want to be left alone."

"Okay, if that's what you want."

After Mardy left, she cried. Laci came back the next day to pick up LaTrish from the hospital. LaTrish had to stay home for at least a week not just for her injury, but from a broken heart. Spencer has caused nothing but pain upon her Mardy wouldn't understand what she was going through. She didn't want to look at a man's face for a while. Ever since she returned back to work, Spencer would be waiting outside for her, but she wouldn't speak to him. He even caught up with her coming out of church on a Sunday. "I know you don't want to talk but can you stop for a minute to hear what I want to say."

"You only have a minute," LaTrish said. "What happened was my fault. I took you through a lot. I would like to pay your hospital bills. She started shaking her head. "I don't need you to."

"Let me do this, at least just as your friend."

"Spencer, I have to go right now."

"Yeah I see Laci coming. I better go before she tackles me. But if you ever need someone to talk to, you know my number." He left. Laci came rushing over. "I know that wasn't Spencer I saw?"

"Yes, it was," LaTrish said. "Lucky we're in the church parking lot, I would of got him in the streets."

Spencer had many sleepless nights because he hasn't heard from LaTrish. One of the nights he was so irritated from not being able to sleep, he was kicking the hell out of his sheets. Then he thought he heard the doorbell ring. He got out of bed and went downstairs. Spencer looked through the peephole. He got angry then opened the door, quick. "Ivori, what are you doing here at 1a.m.?"

"How come you haven't been calling me back or coming by?" she asked. "You know I'm busy all the time and some people have jobs to go to. So, do you mind?"

"I can't stay here tonight?"

"No and how did you get here anyway?"

"I drove my… my baby daddy's car."

"Good night!" Spencer said before he slammed the door. "Spencer!"

The door remained closed. "Forget you anyway," Ivori said then she went back home Spencer went to LaTrish's again but went inside and he sat in the back. Everyone was listening to the sermon. Spencer looked for LaTrish. He couldn't really scope her out because the church was so crowded. Church service ended not long after he got there. Spencer stayed seated to watch who was leaving out the door. He finally saw LaTrish, shaking hands and speaking to people. He didn't want to approach her because he knew Laci had to be there somewhere. Spencer got up and left out of the church. LaTrish was about to get in her car when she noticed a red rose placed underneath one of her windshield wipers. She picked it up looking for a note or who it was from. It didn't matter to her. LaTrish kept staring at the rose. How beautiful it was. Spencer past. She didn't even see him Spencer came home late that night. He tried to turn on the lights, but it wouldn't come on. He kept flicking the switch. When Spencer went further in the house, someone came up behind him and hit him in the back of the head with a vase. He wasn't unconscious, but his vision was blurred. While Spencer was still lying on the floor, he felt something being pierced down in his back, like the barrel of a gun. He tried to get up, but the person said, "if you try to move, I'll shoot you in the back and I mean it!" He couldn't recognize the voice. Spencer knew if he got of this alive, he was going to find out who this was. He got hit in the head again. This time he was out. It was daylight when he woke up. Spencer didn't know if anything has been taken but his house was tore up. He didn't have a clue who could have done this. Spencer called over JD and Willy. He sat down with an ice pack to his head. "Maybe it was someone out of town," JD said. "You don't think it could be somebody from here?" Willy asked. "It could be anybody from Miami to here," Spencer said. "I'm thinking it's that chick Ivori."

"Her! I thought you said it was a guy that attacked you?" JD said. "Yeah she could of set me up and had someone to do the job for her. She's paying me back because I've been blowing her off."

"You should go over there and check her," Willy said. "No, I'm not making it worse than it is. Anyway, I'm just guessing it's her. I don't know for sure."

Friday evening LaTrish cleaned the house and then showered. Her Aunt Bassie, her cousin Laci, and the kids went to Galveston for the weekend. Laci tried persuading her to go to take her mind off of Spencer and everything that's happened. LaTrish wasn't ready for a getaway. "You're lovesick," Laci said to her, "can't live without that man disease. You should be calling that guy that calls here for you."

"Oh Mardy… me and him are just friends."

"You need to let Spencer go. He draws trouble. You see he just got robbed and almost killed."

"I have let him go."

"You can't get him out of your head. That's why you won't get with no one else."

LaTrish paid no attention. LaTrish turned on the TV in her bedroom. Then she headed to the kitchen for something to eat. When she returned to her room, someone came up behind and grabbed her. "Don't hurt me," she said. "I'm not going to hurt you, LaTrish."

She turned around. "Mardy, how did you get in here?" The front door was unlocked. I've been worried about you LaTrish…all what you've been through."

"You heard about Spencer?" LaTrish asked. "What about him?"

"He got attacked in his house this past Sunday night."

"Well he deserved it," Mardy said. "He doesn't deserve to get almost killed."

"A selfish motherfucker like Spencer deserves whatever he gets."

"You're talking about him like you know him," LaTrish said. "I've known Spencer since childhood. We stayed on the same block and went to the same schools. You see, Spencer has always been a cheater. He always skipped school and wanted to use my notes in class and everyone else's homework. That's how he passed every grade. He also stole girlfriends from me. Just like he stole you from me. I was there when you met Spencer. I had seen you first. I acted too shy, so Spencer goes over to you like he's going to talk you into coming over to me, but he decides he wants you for himself. I was heated. I have always hated Spencer. That's what drove me to do what I did."

LaTrish started backing away like she was about to run. Mardy shuts the door so she couldn't go anywhere. "Come on now, let's spend more time together. You're looking all sexy in your lingerie. All this time you've been screwing that bastard, but I can't get any ass for nothing. After all the dates we've been on. Since we're alone it's time you gave me some."

"Mardy please I'm not going to tell anyone about what you did to Spencer."

"I ain't worried. I just want us to get in that bed. I want to see the expression on your face when you're doing me."

LaTrish had to think quick. She played like she was giving into him. They were kissing and rubbing. Then LaTrish kneed him between the legs. He went down holding his stuff. She ran out the room, grabbed the cordless phone, locked herself in the bathroom, and called the police. When she went back to her bedroom, Mardy had disappeared. She had gotten dressed before the police had showed up. After the police left, LaTrish called Spencer. "Hey baby I was wondering when I was going to hear from you," Spencer said. "Listen Spencer, Mardy is the one that tried to kill you."

"How do you know this?"

"He snuck into my house and he told me just know. I called the police, but he got away before they showed up."

"That fool, I should of, known," he said. "Watch your back," LaTrish said. "Did he try to do anything to you?"

"No, not really."

"Not really, huh," Spencer said, "he's going to pay."

Spencer left out of his house. He stood there, looking around. Then he got in his car. When Spencer put his key in the ignition, he felt something on the back of his head. "Well, well, well Spencer where are you heading to?"

"Why do you have to keep threatening me with a gun?"
"I don't have to, I need to. I know the police are looking for me, so my plans are heading to Mexico."

"Then what are you still doing here?"

"I need some money."

"I don't have any," Spencer said. "Yes, you do. I know all about that drug operation you got going on. So, if I go down, you're going with me."

"How much?"

"Ten thousand dollars."

"Ten thousand! That's a lot of money."

"Yeah you're going to write me a check. So, get your ass out."

They go into the house. Spencer went through a drawer and pulled out a checkbook. Mardy had the gun pointed at him when he was writing the check out. Spencer was being a little hesitate. "Will you hurry the hell up! Mardy squealed. When the check was filled out,

Spencer handed it to him. Mardy took it and looked at it. "That's what I'm talking about…ten g's. I'm going to be leaving now and I'm taking LaTrish with me. If you even think about calling the police, I'm going to come back and shoot you for real."

"You stay away from LaTrish," Spencer said. "You can't stop me from doing anything."

Mardy was about to walk out the door but he saw the police pull up through the window. "Ain't this a bitch!"

"What?" Spencer asked. "The police," Mardy answered. "Come here. You're going to get rid of them. No funny business either."

Spencer opened the door. Mardy stayed hid with the gun pointed at Spencer's side. "Spencer Taylor" one of the cops asked. "Yes."

"A man named Mardy Cleaton is believed to be your attempted murderer. Have you come into contact with him again?"

"No, I haven't."

"When we find him, we're going to bring him in for questioning."

"I'll let you know something if I see him," Spencer said. The police left. Mardy peeked through the curtains to be sure they left. Then he took off.

Spencer didn't know where he disappeared to. *He's not going to make it to Mexico,* he said to himself. Spencer left his house and called LaTrish from his cell phone. "You alone?" he asked. "Yes," she answered. "Mardy just left my house. He held me at gun point, demanding money."

"We have to find him before he really hurts somebody," LaTrish said. "He said he was going to Mexico and was taking you with him."

"He hasn't been back over here."

"Well keep on a lookout and I'll get back with you," Spencer said It's fifteen minutes after ten. Mardy had changed clothes and put more clothes in a bag. He crept out the back door of his house. When he walked towards the front, a woman came walking toward him. Mardy didn't know what to think. "Are you Mardy?"

"Who wants to know?"

"I'm Ivori."

"You ain't five-o, are you?"

"Hell no. I was Spencer's other woman. He kicked me to the curb."

"So, what do you want with me?"

"I want you to get him for me. I know you tried to shoot him. You should of killed him."

"Sorry sweetheart, I don't want to have anything to do with anyone that has anything to do with Spencer. "What about his girlfriend LaTrish?"

"That's another story," Mardy said. "So you're not going to help me get Spencer?"

"If you want him so bad, you get him. I'm leaving town." "Can I go where you're going?"

"I don't know you lady. You may not be who you say you are."

"Yes I am. I just want to get out of Baton Rouge like you do. I have nothing to lose."

"When we get to where we're going, I'm going my way and you're going yours," he said. "That's alright with me," Ivori said Laci called LaTrish. "How you're holding up?" Laci asked.

"I'm good."

"You don't sound good. Are you sick or were you hoping I was Spencer calling?"

"I told you I'm not concerned about him."

"Sure, you're not. Well we're all at the hotel getting ready for bed. I was checking up on you. I'll see you when we get back."

"See you later," LaTrish said Mardy and Ivori check into a motel for the night. An hour and a half went by. Mardy goes to sleep. Ivori went to the motel front desk. She was crying and was a mess. "Are you okay?" a man asked. "Can you call the police… I've been raped."

The phone rings seven in the morning, waking LaTrish up. She goes in the living room to answer it. "LaTrish, the police found Mardy," Spencer said. "Really, where?"

"In a motel, dead."

"Dead!"

"Yes, it's all on the news. Somehow the police found him through someone. He did check into a motel room with a woman. Mardy was in the room by himself when the police showed up.

He thought it was the woman knocking at the door at first because he thought she forgot her room key. When he realized it wasn't, Mardy had his gun out. The police kicked in and shot him."

LaTrish was so in shock, she couldn't say anything. "Hello, are you still there LaTrish?"

"Yeah, I just can't believe Mardy is dead."

"Neither can I," Spencer said. Mardy being gone was a shocker all over Baton Rouge. LaTrish felt she's hurting the most because she knew she and Mardy were getting close, but she pushed him away Two weeks later Latrish was getting ready to go out on a Saturday evening on first date in a long time. Laci answered the door when Spencer showed up. When LaTrish was ready, he showed her a bouquet of roses. "How sweet of you," she said. "So where are we going to?"

"To the movies. The same place we went on our very first date."

"Then what are we doing afterwards?"

"We're going back to my place, or our place."

"No, no, no mister. I'm not moving back in."

"I know, I was just playing. You could spend the night."

"I want to take things slow."

"Whatever you want…. Can I least get a kiss?"

They sealed everything with a make-up kiss. As for Ivori, she tried to escape to Mexico with Brownie, the crackhead. Ivori didn't know he had cocaine hidden in the trunk of the Buick they were in and the license plates weren't registered to that vehicle, so the cops pulled them over for under suspicion. They were close but still a long way from Mexico. Now it was someplace they weren't going.

Country Boy, Ghetto Girl

Summer of 1989, an energetic nineteen-year-old, Cristel Browns returns home to her cracker jack box apartment in East St Louis. She just finished a long shift at the Waffle House on an early Friday evening. Cristel lived on her own for only six months with her dead- beat boyfriend and she's already had enough. He'd rather hang out in the streets with his boys than finish college and get a decent job. Just when she was getting relaxed, her boyfriend calls. "What is it, Dexter?"

"I'm in jail."

"What? What happened?"

"I can't talk about it now. Can you come get me out?"

"No because I know it has something to do with those riff raffs you hang out with. Have one of them get you out. Better yet have your parents get you because that's where your stuff is going. When you do get out, don't even think about coming near here because I will get the locks changed."

She ended the conversation there. A couple minutes later the phone rang again. She didn't really want to answer it this time. "Hello!" Cristel said in, anger. "Hello to you too."

"Oh, is this Renee?"

"Long time no hear from," Renee said. "Sorry I didn't mean to be mean."

"I understand. You must have thought I was a bill collector."

"No, I just broke up with my boyfriend."

"Trouble in the man department. I know how that is."

"He's just a boy. He has a lot of growing up to do."

"Being single is the best thing to be sometimes," Renee said. "Why don't you come to Dallas? Take your mind off your ex."

"I can't this weekend."

"How about next weekend?" Renee asked. "That will be better. You're going to take me to Six Flags, right?"

"Yeah, we're family and we're going to kick it like we use to…and Cristel, don't stand me up."

Cristel boarded the Greyhound bus the next Friday about nine o'clock. She sat in the middle of the bus putting on her headphones. Cristel continuously switched back and forth to the R&B and soft rock music stations to stay tuned in with all her favorite songs. Now she was off to Dallas Somewhere in Sweetwater, Texas, a twenty-three-year-old dirty blonde haired stud named Lance Kaysley, just got home from working a graveyard shift. He pulled out some mail from his mailbox. Lance hasn't checked it in the last couple of days, so he had a bundle of mail. Mrs. Bailey from across the street came prancing over. "Hi Lance, I was wondering if you have some cinnamon?"

"No, I certainly don't."

"Oh, too bad. I was going to make some cinnamon pancakes. Guess I'll have to run to the store. Oh shoot, my husband has the car. Would you mind running me by the store?"

"I like to, but I have to get some sleep."

"Oh yeah you work those long hours overnight. No wonder you stay in such great shape. Well thanks anyway." She goes back across the street.

Lance couldn't get over the real tight Mickey Mouse shirt she had on and the daisy dukes that was riding up her butt. The cellulite she had made it worse.

It almost made him nauseated Mid-afternoon, Mrs. Bailey was watering her flowers out front when Lance was about to get into his truck. Hey Lance, can I talk to you for a sec?" she asked, running over to him. "Sure."

"I've grown some vegetables and was wondering if you'd like some?"

"Yeah I'll get some later. Did you ever make it to the store?"

"Yes, Matthew brought the car back from the shop before he went into work."

"I see you got on something different," Lance said. "Matthew bought this dress from Lane Bryant at the Dallas mall you like?"

"I gotta go," he said. Matthew Bailey just pulled up in his patrol car. "Hello hun, I was just about to start dinner."

She ran quickly in the house. Matthew stood there staring at Lance from behind his sunglasses then went in the house too. Lance stopped over at his older sister Lilian's house. He made himself comfortable on the couch. Lilian found him a cigarette and was carrying her one-year-old baby girl. "I thought you quit smoking," she said. "I'm trying to."

"I hope that break up with Sandi isn't bothering you."

"No, I've been past that."

"That was my last cigarette."

"I'll get you some more."

Lilian's husband, Kirk and their other daughter and son just got home. "What's up, Lance?" his brother-in-law said. "Hi uncle Lance," both kids said. Lance just waved and smiled.

"What's been happening with you?" Kirk asked. "Working," Lance answered. "Same here."

"I'm about to head up to Dallas this weekend," Lance said. "Again," Lilian said. "You go up there almost every other weekend."

"There's a lot more going on up there than here. Nobody in this family has ever left Sweetwater, not even our parents. I thought Corey was going to move out to Houston or some other big city, but he rather do drugs and be under that pot head girlfriend he has. I'm too young to be stuck here. I'm going to the convenient store and get you some cigarettes."

"Can you get some mints too?" Lilian asked. The Greyhound bus finally made a stop at a convenient store. "We're now in Sweetwater, Texas. We're only going to take fifteen minutes, only fifteen minutes," the bus driver announced. Cristel went straight to the ladies' room. Lance just pulled up in his truck. A bum was outside in front of the store bothering people. Cristel got some Cheetos, Hostess cupcakes, and a Pepsi after coming from the restroom. It was a long line of people when she got in line. Lance got a beer, got the mints, and waited in line to buy some cigarettes. He was standing behind Cristel. The line went pretty quickly but when Cristel headed towards the bus, the bum started harassing her. "I don't have any extra change, I don't have nothing for you."

He took her bag from her. "Give me my bag!"

"Give me some change! I haven't eaten in weeks!"

"You just want some liquor money."

He took a bite out of one of her cupcakes. "You fool!" Cristel screamed. "Leave her alone," Lance said. "You're always out here bothering folks. Get somewhere."

Cristel took her bag back. Then she saw her bus go down the road. "No, I can't believe this is happening! My stuff! How am I going to get to Dallas now?"

"You're heading to Dallas?" Lance asked. "I was."

"I can take you there. I was going there anyway."

"No thank you. I'll wait on another bus."

"Another bus isn't going to come for another fourteen hours."

"I'm going to find a payphone," Cristel said. "There's one on this side of the building but it might be broke."

Cristel used the payphone but didn't get a dial tone. Lance was standing against his truck waiting for her to make a decision. "I need to find a phone desperately."

"When you find a phone, then what?"

"I'm just going to tell my cousin I'm going to be arriving later."

"How was you going to get there?" Lance asked. "I guess…I guess I'll ride with you."

He opened the passenger door for her. "Was you really going to Dallas?" she asked, after he got in. "Yes."

"Is it a long drive?"

"Yeah, but I go up there twice a month."

"Really."

He nodded his head. "I'll take you to a phone. My brother's house is on the way we're headed."

Lance made a stop back at Lilian's house right after they left the convenient store. "I'll be right back," he said. He came back ten minutes later. As they continued on, he asked, "where you from?"

"St. Louis."

"You like it there?"

"It's okay."

Lance stopped back at his house. "I have to go in and get some stuff. You might want to come in. It's too hot to sit out here."

"Where are we?" Cristel asked. "This is my place."

"We're really not going to Dallas, are we?"

"Why you ask that?" Lance asked. "You said you were taking me to a phone."

"I am. There's one in here."

"What are you getting out of this? What do you care if I get to Dallas or not?"

"I've told you already," he said. "You said you had a brother, we were going to his house to use the phone."

"I forgot I needed some things to take with me, so I stopped here."

"I'm not getting out."

Lance left her in the truck. He came right back out. "Will you get out of the truck?"

"No. You don't even have a brother, do you?"

"Yes, I do. His phone don't even be on half the time anyway. That's why I'm glad I came back home."

"I'll wait."

"Look if you don't want your cousin to be worried about you, you need to get in here and use this phone."

Matthew was looking out the window from across the street. "I'm going to go pack some stuff," Lance said, "there's the phone. Cristel stood by the door of his living room. He came back through the living room and Cristel was still standing by the door. "Did you ever talk to your cousin?"

"Not yet."

"Why haven't you?"

"I just want to go back to St. Louis."

"You don't want to do that. You came all this way. I'm going to see you get to Dallas."

"Why are you trying so hard?"

"Because I'm a nice guy."

He left the room to finish packing. She called Renee. "What on Earth are you doing in Sweetwater?"

"I got stranded here, but someone is bringing me to Dallas."
"Somebody you know?"

"No just someone."

"Just be careful. Get here safely and soon."
"I will."

"Ready to go?" Lance asked. "Yes," Cristel answered. Matthew came over when they just walked outside. "You heading somewhere?" he asked. "Lance answered. "I have something to ask you… are you hitting on my wife?"

"Hitting on your wife… what do you mean?"

"I've been noticing some flirting going on."

"Maybe she's flirting with me."

"Maybe. Maybe it's the other way around."

"She's the one always coming over in my yard."

"Please, you probably whistled her over here."

"Matthew, I don't want to get into it with you. I have to go."

"You just remember I'm watching you."

He went back over across the street Lance and Cristel went on their way. Cristel kept staring at Lance. He was being very quiet while driving. He kept his eyes on the road then finally asked, "what?"

"I was just wondering what kind of man are you? You're checking out married women. I was wondering, what are your intentions with me?"

"I do not mess with married women."

"What was you planning on getting out of taking me to Dallas? You're not getting a taste of my cookie if that's what you're thinking."

"For your information, you're really not my type," he said. "Oh, why are you taking me to Dallas?"

"You ask the same questions."

"You could be a convict or a rapist."

"If I was a rapist I would of did you by now."

"You wouldn't dare."

"Why wait?"

"Yeah, you probably was planning on taking me out in the middle of nowhere and have your way with me. Let me out of this truck."

"No."

"Let me out!"

"We are out on the road."

"Let me out of this freaking truck!" Lance pulled over real quick. "You want out, get out."

Cristel didn't move. "What are you waiting on?" he asked. "I didn't mean right here, I meant like an exit off the highway."

"Well you're getting off right here."

"No this is dangerous."

"Well you should of thought about that before you yelled at me."

Cristel shook her head. "Get your crazy ghetto ass out of my truck."

"Oh no you did not say that but I'm still not getting out."

"Oh, we'll see about that."

Lance took off and left her on the side of the road. "Forget you anyway country boy!" Cristel walked on. She tied up her shirt then hung her purse around herself. The sun was beating down on her. She grabbed her Pepsi out of her plastic bag but didn't want to drink it because it was no bathrooms around. *This is nuts! What kind of man would leave a woman on the side of the road? What am I going to do? I'm not going to make it nowhere by walking. Maybe I can catch a ride back to the bus station.* Cars and trucks kept passing her by. Surely enough, somebody in a transman pulled over. When Cristel walked up to the passenger side she saw a spiked hair guy that almost scared her. "Where you heading?" he asked. "Dallas."

"Wow you're a long way from there."

"My car broke down. Can you drop me off at a gas station or something?"

"Hop in."

She got in. They sped off. He was blasting Guns N' Roses song "Welcome to the Jungle," and was singing along. *What did I get myself into?* she asked herself. "Where are you from? You don't sound like you're from around here," the man asked. "The Midwest."

"You were traveling all this way by yourself?" Next thing, they heard someone honking. He looked in his rearview mirror. "Who the heck is this?" Cristel turned around. Lance was following them. He continued to honk. "Who is this maniac?" He merged into the left lane. Lance moved over into the left lane too. He moved back to the right lane. Lance stayed on him. The man sped up. "Please slow down," Cristel said. Lance honked like crazy. The man pulled over. Lance got out of his truck. The man got out the car.

"Who the fuck are you, and what is your problem?" Lance told Cristel to get out of the car. "No, you left me," she said. "Please get out of the car."

She stayed put with her arms folded. "I don't know what's going on but you two better get the hell on!" Cristel got out of the car.

"Last time I'm picking up anybody," the man said and drove away. "How could you do that to me? Leave me out in the heat!"

"I just did that because I was mad," Lance said. "I wasn't going to really leave you stranded."

"But still how was I going to know?" Cristel said. She started walking away. "Where are you going?"

"I'm going to find a way back to the bus stop."

"No come on, get in the truck."

"No, you left me out in this heat. I'll find my own way to Dallas."

Lance grabbed her arm. She snatched her arm from him. "Sorry I didn't mean to do that," Lance said. "I'll take you to Dallas. I brought you this far."

He had the passenger door opened for her. Cristel started to get in but she kicked him between the legs. "I'm sorry I didn't mean to kick you so hard."

He had a hold on his privates like he was in great pain. Cristel quickly realized he was faking. She ran. Lance ran after her. "Stay away from me!" she screamed. "Get back here!" he shouted. Cristel kept running but was about to slip off the edge of the cliff. She stepped on a rock, then stumbled over the edge.

"Hey!" Lance yelled. He climbed his way down to her. "Get away from me!" She was lying on the ground with a few scrapes. "What is wrong with you? I'm trying to help you."

"I don't want your help."

"Fine you want to cry about being left in the heat, go ahead and die in the heat."

A state trooper passing through saw Lance's truck on the side of the road. He got out of the patrol car and seen them below. "What are you two doing down there?" Lance helped Cristel up the little cliff. "Sorry, she fell."

"How did she fall?"

"I got car sick," Cristel said, quickly. "I got out the truck, started throwing up on the side of the road, not knowing I was too close to the edge. I ended up stumbling down the cliff."

"I see," the trooper said. "You alright?"

"Yes sir."

"You kids be careful out here and have a nice day."

"You do the same," Lance said. The trooper took off.

Lance and Cristel got in the truck. He stared at her then started laughing. "What are you laughing at?"

"You are really something else. I never got your name."

"You never told me your name either," Cristel said. "I'm Lance."

Cristel was just sitting there not saying anything. "And you are?" he asked. "Cristel," she finally said. "You hungry, Cristel?"

"Yeah, and I'm smelly and I feel yucky. I need something to change into, but all my stuff is gone."

"Let's start off by getting something to eat," Lance said. They stopped at a diner in the middle of nowhere. Cristel took big bites of her cheeseburger and was stuffing herself with the fries. "Hungry, aren't we?" Lance asked. She continued to eat. "You have a boyfriend?"

"Why do you ask?"

"You seem to always give men a hard time or do you just give me a hard time?"

"I don't have a boyfriend. We broke up recently. Nothing against you."

Cristel's stomach started hurting. She thought it was because she hadn't eaten in a long time. Cristel rushed to the bathroom. Her stomach cramped even more. She ended up starting her period.
After being in the bathroom for five minutes, Cristel came out saying to Lance, "I need to go to the nearest store or convenient store soon as possible."

They managed to run into a Wal-Mart. Lance walked around while Cristel was picking out what she needed. Lance waited up front but grew impatient because she took a long time. "Was you trying to buy up the whole store?" he asked after they finally left. "Sorry, I had things to get."

"I'm tired and it's getting late. We're going to stay at my brother's place for the night then continue on in the morning."

"I got to call my cousin back and tell her."

"You can do that. You can also get cleaned up if you want," Lance said. Lance's younger brother Corey was peeking out his front window of his house when they pulled up. "Look who decides to show up," Corey said after he came out with his arms up in the air. "I just wanted to see what my little brother was up to and I was on my way to Dallas, so I wondered if we could stay the night before we headed there."

"We... who's we?" Corey asked. They looked toward Lance's truck which Cristel was waiting. "Who's that?"

"Someone I brought with me."

"She's not a cop, is she?"

"No. Stop worrying. Every stranger that comes by you have a doubt about because of what you're growing in your backyard."

"No, I don't. You and your friend can spend the night."

"Cool," Lance said. He gets Cristel and they get their stuff out of the truck. Cristel starts coughing once they walk through the front door. "You two be forever smoking weed."

Corey's girlfriend, Andrea, was sitting on the couch smoking away. "Can you show this young lady where she's going to sleep at?" Corey asked Andrea. She was so high she didn't hear him. "Would you please come off of cloud nine and show our company where she can sleep at tonight."

"Damn, you ain't got to be fucking disturbing me!" Andrea said. "Don't use that language and do what I asked."

Cristel followed Andrea to a back room. "Is your phone working?" Lance asked. "Yeah. Your little friend is kind of hot. You guys want to smoke a little something, something?"

"No, I don't do that, and I doubt she does either."

"How about a drink?" Corey asked. "Like a Miller Light or something?"

"I'll take that," Lance said. Cristel comes back. "You smoke or anything?" Corey asked her. "No."

"Drink?"

"No, I'm not twenty-one yet."

"So I won't tell if you don't tell."

Corey got them both Miller Lights. "Could I use your phone?" Cristel asked. "Go ahead," Corey said. She used the phone sitting on the living room table. "My goodness… where the heck are you?" Renee asked. "You got me worried."

"I didn't mean to worry you, but I'm fine. I'm staying over someone's house for the night. I'll be there in the morning I promise."

"What are you up to? Are you involved in something?"

"No. It was getting late, and he was tired so… "He! So, you letting strange men pick you?"

"Renee! The bus I was suppose, to have rode down there left me. I had no choice but to accept a ride from someone who was kind enough to bring me where I needed to get to."

"You're not here yet."

"I know. I'll be there in the morning."

Renee hung up. The other three were talking. Lance pulled out the conversation when he seen the expression on Cristel's face when she got off the phone."

"Everything okay?" he asked. "She's mad at me. I want to take a shower and go to sleep."

Corey and Andrea smoked their blunts, staying in their world. Cristel takes her shower Lance was sitting in a chair in the bedroom watching the news, when she finished her shower. "Feel better?" he asked. "A little. I'll feel even better when I get some sleep."

She laid down on the bed. "I didn't mean to bring you around these pot heads. I didn't think you want to be in a motel. My apologies."

A knock was on the bedroom door. "You kids alright in here?" Corey asked. "Yeah, we're fine," Lance said. Corey laid a couple of condoms on the dresser. "What are you doing?" Lance asked. "Just in case. You know AIDS is a big issue now these days. Goodnight."

"Nobody's using condoms in here," Lance said, and he put them away in the dresser drawer. "You have other family in Dallas other than your cousin?" he asked. "I have family all over Texas but I'm not close to any of them except her."

"What about in St. Louis? You have brothers and sisters, or parents that live there?"

"My father and mother, no siblings. My cousin Renee was like my big sister. I feel alone when she's not with me. You have a wife, girlfriend, or children?"

"No, none of the above. At least not yet. I know you want to get some sleep, so I'll be out here sleeping on the couch if you need me."

"Goodnight and thank you," Cristel said. She rolls over and drifts off to sleep. Three in the morning, Lance was snoozing away until some noises woke him up. The noises were coming from his brother's room. "You got to be kidding me," Lance said. He hopped up from the couch and screamed, "you guys cut out all that noise! You shouldn't be fucking when you have company and interrupting people's sleep."

Corey stuck his head out his bedroom door. "My bad… I'll be more quiet."

Lance laid back down. Lance was up seven sharp. He loaded his baggage in his truck. Corey came outside. "How'd you sleep?"

"I slept fine, thank goodness. I hope Cristel didn't hear you guys."

"How long you're going to be in Dallas?"

"Two days at least."

"On your way back from Dallas, you and I should head up to Houston because I have an amigo that know some people up there that can hook us up with some good stuff."

"No," Lance said. "I have a job to get back to and a job I want to keep. You need to get a job and leave that stuff alone and stop living off of disability checks, knowing you ain't disabled."

"I am handicapped and I'm never going to stop doing drugs."

A police car passed through, turned around and stopped. "Oh shit," Corey said. Matthew Bailey and another police officer stepped out of the car. "What are you doing here?" Lance asked. "Well you are under arrest."

"For what?"

"Sexual assault."

"Who did I sexually assault?"

"You sexually assaulted my wife."

"That's a lie. Your wife chases after every young guy she sees. "She told me you talked her into coming over to your place. You were saying dirty things and touching her the wrong way. She's been afraid to tell me until now."

"This all made up. You don't want to accept the fact that your wife is a slut."

Matthew turned red. "Cuff him," he told the other officer. He handcuffed Lance. "Get the keys out of my pocket," Lance said to Corey. Corey reached in his pocket, got the keys out. "You're going to have to take Cristel to Dallas."

"I don't know about that," Corey said. "Somebody's got to do it."

The police officer put Lance in the back of the police car. Cristel came out asking, "what's going on?" Matthew and the other cop got in and drove away. "Lance just got arrested," Corey said. He placed the keys in her hand. "Sorry but you're on your own."

An hour went by. Cristel stayed in the room wondering what she was going to do. She certainly wasn't calling Renee to tell her anything. "This is the most tripped out road trip I've ever been on."

Cristel heard Corey talking on the phone after it rung a couple times. She knew he had to be talking to Lance because he said, "don't worry we'll get you out." Then Corey came in the room. "Telephone for you."

"Lance! What happened?"

"I just got arrested by this punk ass cop who's accusing me of something because he doesn't like me. What you might need to do is drive yourself to Dallas…can you do that?"

"Yeah I know how to get there. But what about you?"

"Don't worry about me. I'm getting out. I just don't want to hold you up. Besides I didn't want my brother or his girl taking you anyway as high as they get. Soon as you get to Dallas, call me. I'll catch up with you later. You got the keys?" Lance asked. "Yes," Cristel said. "Go ahead and go."

Cristel got all her stuff, told Corey and Andrea that she was out of here. Finally, she hit the road.

Cristel was enjoying her ride. It was peaceful and breezy. It gave her time to think. Then she thought it was too quiet for her. She flipped through the radio stations trying to find an R&B station. A Prince song, "Scandalous," was on. Then the rapper MC Hammer came on. She didn't care for him too much, so she changed the station. Cristel came across the rock station and George Michael's song, "Father Figure," just came on. She cut it up and was grooving to it. After that song was over she was hoping they weren't going to play something she didn't care to hear. Madonna's song, "La Isla Bonita," came on next. "She's cool," Cristel said. She partied to every hit she heard to keep her in a pleasant mood until she reached her destination Corey and a Hispanic friend of his named Pedro picked Lance up. Come to find out it was all a misunderstanding. Mrs. Bailey came down to the police station to tell Matthew that Lance could never do that. He's too nice of a guy. As much as Matthew didn't want to release him, but he did. "I think she's screwing some man," Lance said. "He just wanted to accuse me because she always eyed me."

"So, what are you going to do now?" Corey asked. "Is that Honda of yours still running?"

"It needs an alternator."

"Man, I need to get to Dallas."

"My man Pedro can take us there."

"Really. I give you money, you take me to Dallas?"

"Sure, no problem my friend. You show me the money I'll take you where ever you need to go."

"Will thirty dollars do?"

"Si."

"Shit give me some money," Corey said. "You just want to smoke it up," Lance said. "Like he ain't."

Pedro giggled as he put the money in his pocket. Cristel got to Renee's house before noon. Renee was just coming out of the house. She gave Cristel a big hug. When she let go of her, Cristel could swear Renee was crying. "Is something wrong?" Cristel asked. "I didn't know what to think. I was scared something might of happened to you or I was afraid you decided not to come because of what I said the last time we talked."

"Nothing was going my way getting down here. But I'm here now and I'm glad. I'm glad I made it here on my own."

"Who's truck is that?"

"A friend let me use it to get here."

"That man you was talking about? Girl you move fast. Broke up with one then got you another one."

"It's not like that. He really helped me out. As of matter of fact… I have to call him."

Cristel ran into the house and got on the phone. She let it ring several times before she decided to give up. "Any luck?" Renee asked. "Nobody's home. I hope…"

"You hope what?" Cristel just walked away. Pedro, Lance, Corey, and Andrea were riding in Pedro's van. Corey and Andrea were in the back making out. Lance turned around because they were disturbing him. "You guys are not in a hotel. Nobody wants to keep seeing you two screw around."

"Then turn around," Corey said. "I still can hear you."

"I hope when we get to Dallas you get you some."

"I'm not going up there for that."

"Why not? You let her drive your truck and maybe you'll stop hating so much."

"You think I'm hating on you two?"

"Yes, and another thing…I hope you know where to find her."

"Of course. She told me everything."

"Okay just make sure you get a piece."

Renee and Cristel went to the mall. Renee's mother was putting together a party at her house. Renee knows her mama likes putting together fancy events. Which meant they had to get something nice to wear. Cristel fell in love with this silk thin-strapped, golden colored dress in the first clothing store they walked in to. She tried it on. It fit perfectly. It even helped her chest stand out more. Renee tried on almost everything in store. Cristel's mind wandered while waiting on Renee to decide on what dress to buy. She kept thinking about Lance. They went to a carnival after spending two hours in the mall.

Renee has noticed every time she asks Cristel something, she doesn't answer until five minutes later. "Earth to Cristel. Please come back from planet Pluto, or is it Jupiter?"

"Girl my mind is just on something else."

"That man?" Renee asked. "You never did tell me the story on you and him and how you ended up driving up here alone in his truck."

"It's a long story. It's not that he's a bad person or anything."

"Is he coming back for his truck?"

"Yes."

"Does he know where to find it?"

"He says he does. He knows Dallas well. I made sure he got the directions to where I'm staying. Wait a minute! What if he's on his way to Dallas right now? We better get back to the house," Cristel said. "Hold up," Renee said. "First, I want to ride a few rides and have some funnel cake."

"I'm with that," Cristel said. It was near seven in the evening when they were getting ready for the party. "What's this guy like, that you're secretly involved with?" Renee asked, sitting in front of a mirror, pinning up her hair. "I'm not involved with him. He's nice."

Renee put some lip gloss on. "Is he tall, dark, and handsome?"

"He's handsome."

"What is he light skinned, caramel skinned?"

"He's white."

Renee's eyes got big. "He's who?"

"White."

"You were with a white guy?"

"Is that a problem?"

"No, not at all."

Cristel stepped outside for some fresh air. She couldn't stop thinking about Lance. If he even gotten out of jail. Cristel was thinking about getting back in the truck and driving back to Sweetwater but then she thought, he'll get here. A few minutes later, a van pulled up behind Lance's truck. Lance got out the passenger side of the van. Lance, she said on the inside. Cristel wanted to burst but she knew she had to keep it under control. "I see you made it," he said. "Yeah, and so did you," she said. Corey, Andrea, and Pedro got out of the van. "Let me get your key."

Cristel went in the house. "Mama sita," Pedro said to Lance. "What are you doing?" Renee asked, when Cristel came back in the house. "He's outside."

Cristel got his key out of her purse. She went outside with Cristel but Renee stayed on the stayed on the front steps. "Wow another mama sita," Pedro said. She gave him the key. "You're going out?" Lance asked. "Yeah, my aunt is having a party at her house."

"How long you're planning on staying at the party?"

"Not too long. Why? "Maybe we can do something before it gets too late."

"What you have in mind?"

"You'll see and be sure to wear that dress."

"What are you about to get into?"

"We're about to check into a hotel and they want to go out to a club."

"Well I can't wait to see what you got planned."

"I can't wait either," Lance said. They gave each other I want you so bad stare. Cristel whispered in his ear, "I missed you when we were apart. I want to kiss you."

"Why don't you?" Lance asked. "Everybody's watching."

"And."

They kissed. They kissed for a long time. Renee was like, "wow."

"I don't mean to interrupt your love scene, but we're here to see Dallas not to see you smooch," Corey said. "Look who's talking," Lance said. "I'll see you say, around eleven," he asked Cristel. "Yeah, eleven," she agreed. They kissed real quick. Lance and the others left. Cristel went up the steps. "What do you think?" she asked Renee. "He's handsome," Renee said Matthew just got home. He heard his wife in the bedroom, laughing. He also heard someone else. He grabbed his rifle from the closet. Matthew crept to the bedroom door. He slowly opened the door. A young red-head man jumped out of the bed. Mrs. Bailey just hid herself behind the covers. "What the hell you doing in my house?" The man was just standing there shaking and butt naked. "I was just…I was just…"

"You were just fucking my wife."

Matthew pointed the rifle at him. "Get out of here before I murder your ass!" He picked up his clothes and ran. Matthew then pointed the rifle at his wife. "Whore, I should of known."

"Go ahead. Shoot me. You make me want to die."

He kept one eye closed, wanting to pull the trigger. He went outside instead, got in his patrol car and drove away. Mrs. Bailey jumped in her robe and tried to see which way he went. She couldn't because he was long gone. Cristel was back on the bus Monday morning to St. Louis. What a weekend she thought as she got comfortable in her seat. After what all has happened, she was glad to have met a guy like Lance. After her aunt's party, he took her to his favorite spot to eat. They had crab legs which was the first time she had them. The dessert there was scrumptious. That was it, from there. Cristel thought he was going to want something but he was a gentleman. It would have been just a weekend thing. She didn't see him anymore after that. Sunday, she spent the whole day with Renee and her aunt. Renee told her to consider moving to Dallas. Cristel said that is something she's definitely doing in the future. She was glad to be back to good ole' St. Louis after that long journey. As Cristel walked through the bus station, she saw a man that looked like Lance. It seemed like he was waiting on someone. He saw her and smiled. "Lance," she said. "You had nice ride?" he asked. "It was long. How did you know when I was going to get here?"

"Your cousin Renee told me what time you were going to arrive here. I thought since I wanted to see St, Louis and I knew someone who could show me around---"

"You are amazing," Cristel said, "to come all this way."

"I want us to continue what we started," Lance said, "not have a memory of some weekend."

"Lance, we live a ways from each other."

"Yeah but that can change. Have you considered moving to the south?"
"Not in Sweetwater."

"I know you've thought about moving to Dallas. I'm definitely moving to Dallas," Lance said.

"Renee told you I was moving to Dallas, didn't she?"
"Something like that."

Cristel put her arms around his neck. "How about we continue right now?"

"How about later? Too many people watching," he said. "And," Cristel said. They kissed while people looked and walked by. But neither one didn't care.

The Season to Love

Millian Starks was a thirty-five-year-old who worked at a Kinder Care Learning Center with Donesha Ronaldson. They just finished up their day and were getting ready to get into their cars and home. "One more week and it's Christmas break." Donesha said.

"Thank you, Jesus. I'm in need of a break," Millian said. "See ya Monday."

Millian, whom is often called Milly, worked in South Kansas City, Missouri and lived in South Kansas City. She attended Longview Community College right after high school for two years. Studying to be a teacher has always been her goal. Milly adored small children. That's why Kindergarten has been the only grade level she's taught for thirteen years. Donesha has been her friend since Kindergarten. Donesha also does hair on the side for a living. Christmas vacation time finally came around. Milly was relaxing in her easy chair on a Friday evening, looking through a Victoria Secret's catalogue. The phone rang. She wasn't in no rush to pick up the phone. "I was just about to hang up. I didn't think you were at home but I'm glad you're there because I have some news for you," Donesha said. "What is it?"

"Milli Vanilli you are going to love what I'm going to tell you."

"Donesha will you tell me."

"Larry is coming back."

"Larry…Larry Spooner?" Milly asked. "Yes. He's finally getting out of the military and staying for good."

"Really. How did you find this out?"

"His sister Arlene. I ran into her at the Oak Park Mall this past Saturday. She asked if you and I would like to come by her house on Monday because he is stopping by there."

"I can't wait," Milly said. "Well you're going to have to. Monday is just three days away."

"I know. I'm going to be counting down the days."

"Yeah, you do that. I'll talk to you tomorrow," Donesha said. "Tomorrow," Milly said. After Milly got off the phone, she ran into the bathroom and looked in the mirror. *I have to fix myself up,* she told herself. Milly has had a crush on Lawrence Spooner since the sixth grade. He was so smart and so cute then. He still was as a grown man but handsome. She hasn't seen him in three years, but Milly knows he's more good-looking now than ever. Larry has always been a good friend to her throughout the years. He was also very popular in high school. Larry played basketball, did the morning announcements his senior year and even was crowned prom king. Every girl wanted him. Milly knew she wouldn't stand a chance against those other girls. She didn't think she was as pretty. She wasn't popular either, but Larry always acknowledged her when other guys didn't. Because of her low self-confidence, Milly accepted to go out with this boy who was a junior and she was a sophomore at the time. He had poor attendance which drew what kind of future he wanted for himself, but Milly didn't care because she was glad someone was interested in her. Their relationship ended soon because she believed she gave it up too soon or he didn't care about her in the first place. He obviously didn't care about his education anyway either. So, she had to get over it and move on. Larry had a scholarship to go to college but, he chose not to go because his mother suffered a stroke. No one else was around to take care of her so he did. Larry's parents been divorced since he was fourteen. A couple years after his mother recovered from her stroke, he enlisted in the Army. He stayed in it for three years in Germany then he came back home. Milly was afraid he was going to end up with a wife and some kids by now. Every time she seen him he had a different lady. By 2008, he went back into the service and now another three years has passed and he's staying for good. This was her chance. Her chance to tell him how much she's been in love with him all these years. Saturday. She and Donesha spent all day shopping. Sunday. Milly went to church and ate dinner at her parents' house. When Sunday came to a close, Milly was too excited to go to sleep. She put in a Beyonce CD. She danced around her bedroom, tidied up her bed, slipped on her nightgown, then she brushed her teeth, flossed, and gargled. Her favorite track came on, "Sweet Dreams."

It made her think about Larry. It made her want to close her eyes and dream away. Milly laid down on her bed and relaxed to the music until the last song played. She got up and turned off her CD player. Milly went to the bathroom and came out a minute later. She couldn't believe what she was seeing. Larry was sitting on her bed, shirtless, with just silk pajama pants on. He was smiling and waiting on her. He said, "come here."

Is he really talking to me? There's nobody here but me. She climbed on top of him and they started kissing. He rolled over on top of her and said, "I've been waiting for this moment for a long time."

"This is too good to be true," Milly said. Milly jumped up out of bed because her CD was scratching. She turned off CD player then she went to use the bathroom. Milly came out a minute later. There was no one in her bed. She knew it was a just a dream…but a sweet dream. She climbed in her quiet lonely bed and turned off the light. "Have a seat," Arlene said, when Donesha and Milly got to her house. "Larry just called, said he's going to be here shortly. While we're waiting on him, Larry and I have this Christmas party we're putting together, and I want you two to come."

"Sure, we'd love to come. We need to bring anything?" Donesha asked. "It doesn't matter…something to drink or maybe some plastic ware. I'm so excited to see my baby brother. He's been gone three years. He's going to be happy to see you ladies too."

"Especially Milly," Donesha said. Milly blushed. A knock was at the door. Arlene peeks out the window then answered the door. "Lawrence!"

"Hey sis!" They gave each other big hugs. Then she stood back and looked at him. "Look at you. Looking all good in your uniform…oh remember Donesha and Milly."

"Yeah, long time no see."

Larry held out his hand. Donesha shook it, then Milly did. Milly didn't want a handshake. She preferred a hug. He was so much more gorgeous than ever. "You found yourself a place or are you staying at mama's?"

"I'm going to stay with Mama for now. I brought somebody with me."

"Really, who?" Larry stood in the doorway and waved the person to come in. A long-haired beauty came in. "This is Kieha. She's from Maui."

"Hello," Kieha said. "This my sister Arlene."

"Lawrence has told me so much about you."

"Kieha these two ladies I've known almost my whole life."

She looked at Donesha and Milly but didn't say anything to them. "Lawrence why don't you show your sister the pictures."

"I think I left my phone in the car," he said. "How long you two been knowing each other?" Arlene asked. "We've been together for two years," Kieha said. "We fell in love the first time we laid eyes on each other." She laid a big kiss on him. Milly looked at Donesha. "I'm ready to leave."

"We have somewhere to run to. Thanks for inviting us over," Donesha said. "Thanks," Milly said to Arlene. "Oh, thank you. Don't forget about the Christmas party."

"We won't. Nice seeing Larry," Milly said. "Nice seeing you too."
Kieha looked at them in a fierce way when they walked out the door. "Can you believe that hussy?" Donesha asked as soon as they got in the car. "No, I can't," Milly said. "Giving us looks and don't speak. Who do she think she is? You can tell by the way she looks she must be one of those rich stuck up people. Yeah, one of those spoiled kids that never worked a day in her life. Look how flawless she looked.

I think she knew one of us have a crush on him. That's why she kissed him. I hope Larry isn't planning on spending the rest of his life with her. Milly relaxed, her mind wandering. "Please say something," Donesha said.

"What is there to say. They're in love."

"How do you know he's in love with her? He didn't even kiss her back."

"They've been together for two years."

"He probably just needed someone to be with, being away from home for so long," Donesha said. "Donesha he brought her back home. A man is not going to bring a woman home that he has had just a fling or an affair with. When a man brings a woman home, what does that tell you?" Donesha said nothing. Milly was in a daze all day. She couldn't even sleep for nothing that night. The man she always had loved, loves another. Milly could see them now. Having fun in the bedroom. She started having a fantasy of herself and Larry in a beautiful garden, nude like Adam and Eve. There were no worries because nothing in this garden was forbidden. They fed each other all the delicious fruit. They made love in the garden and under the waterfalls of passion. A dream so good, it helped her go to sleep Larry had just placed some wood in the fireplace. Kieha sat on the floor beside him then started kissing him on the neck. "We can't do any of that," he said. "Why not?"

"We're not married. That's why we have to sleep in separate rooms. My mother's rules."

"We can't cuddle?"

"Of course we can cuddle."

"Everything's going to change when we get our place the first of the year. I found the perfect spot for us," Kieha said. "What's the name of that area on the side of the state line?"

"Leawood or Johnson County," Larry said. "I got to get a job."

She put her arms around him. "You don't have to worry about that now. My daddy is gonna pay for our place. "I'm a grown man. Men are suppose to work for what they want."

"Well this money is going to help us out until you find something."

Milly and her mother Karla did what was left of their Christmas shopping on a Tuesday afternoon. "This is it for me. No more shopping," Karla said when they sat down in the food court. Milly took a little box out of her Macy's bag to look at the ring she bought herself. "That ring is really beautiful," Karla said. "You should check out this new Wonder Bra I bought at Victoria Secret's."

"I'm sure it's nice…Milly when are you going to get married?"

"I don't know."

"Your father and I've been married for thirty-six years. You're thirty-five, have no children, no husband…do you even have a man?"

"Mama why are we talking about this?"

"Are you happy?"

"Yes, I'm happy with the way I am can we drop the subject?"

"I'm just asking because you're an attractive woman with a good job and a good education. I'm wondering why are you choosing to be alone?"

"I'm hungry I'm going to get something to eat."

Milly walked around to see what she wanted to eat. She chose Charley's Grill. Milly stepped up to the order here spot when it was her turn to order. She ordered the buffalo chicken combination with a strawberry lemonade. When Milly was paying the man at the register, she couldn't help notice the guy that was in front of her at first looked like Larry but she didn't want to look over at him to see if it was. "Milly," the man said, that was ahead of her in line She looked over at him. "Larry."

"I thought that was you," Larry said. "You Christmas shopping?" he asked. "Yeah, I just finished it."

"I'm just starting. I just had to get something to eat. I didn't have breakfast this morning."

He had two sandwiches, two fries, and two drinks on his tray.

"You must be really hungry or you eating with someone?"

"Yeah, me and Kieha are about to do some shopping."

Speaking of Kieha, she came over. "Kieha you remember Milly when she was at my sister's house?" Kieha didn't respond. She gave Milly the same look the last time. "Did you get the napkins and straws?" Kieha asked Larry. "I got everything."

"We got a lot of shopping to do," she said. "Bye, Milly," he said as they walked away. Milly went back to her table with her tray of food. Karla was looking at her frowny face. "Oh, I didn't mean to upset you," her mother said, holding her hand. "I'm not upset."

After Milly said that she saw Larry and Kieha all close at a table not far from them. "You know what... I'm ready to go. I'm just going to carry my sandwich and get out of here."

Milly didn't want to think or fantasize about Larry. She said her prayers and went on to sleep. Wednesday Milly got up early. She was thinking about Starbucks so she went there. She had a seat and enjoyed her caramel apple spice latte Milly brought a Black Hair magazine to flip through. She was thinking about a look she wanted Donesha to give her. "Well it seems we keep running into each other."

Milly looked up. "Hi Larry," she said, without any enthusiasm. "May I sit with you?"

"Go ahead. Where's your girlfriend? Is she around?"

"No, she doesn't like getting up early. I take it you don't really care for her?"

"Is she always rude or is she only like that with me?"

"She's not bad…she's…not a people person."

"Oh," Milly said. "I'm sorry if she seemed rude."

Milly drank up her latte. "So, what's been going on, old friend? How's life?" Larry asked. "Good," she said. "You seeing anybody, are you married?"

"No to both."

"I can't see how you're single. You look good."

"Nobody wants to commit these days. Especially when you're independent woman. I was engaged once, but he wanted to be possessive over me."

"You have any kids?" Larry asked. "Definitely not. I'm thinking about getting back into traveling. I been nowhere in two years."

"Have you ever been to Hawaii?"

"No."

"You should go. Make that your next place to visit."

"I would like to, but I wouldn't want to go to a place like Hawaii, alone."

"You shouldn't let that stop you. I've went to one of the most beautiful, exotic, romantic place in the world all by myself."

"That's only because you were in the service then you met somebody and then brought that little souvenir back with you."

"I know she's harsh but she's helping me out. She's helping me get a job because she knows people. I was never good at getting anything on my own."

"How can you say that? You were smart, popular in school."

"My looks made me popular. That's the only reason girls wanted to be with me. Milly you were so different from the other girls. So quiet and sweet."

"I thought you were too popular to notice."

"No, I noticed. I was really hoping we would be together. I just didn't want those girls to be mad at you."

She couldn't believe it. Milly thought she was dreaming again. Nope those words actually came from his lips which she wanted to kiss right now. Then his cell phone rang. It was an Alicia Keys ring tone which Milly loved. "Where are you?" Kieha asked. "I'm at Starbucks."

"It takes you that long to get something from Starbucks?"

"I didn't think it mattered. You wasn't up yet."

"You hurry up and get back here with the car you hear me!" She hung up. "Well I gotta run. It was good chatting with you."

"You too," Milly said. Milly shook her head after Larry left. "How pathetic. He runs when she calls. Spoiled my damn moment. She's like a thunderstorm that ruins your pretty day. I hate that bitch."

"I don't understand it. I thought Larry was better than that," Milly said while she Donesha was at Barnes and Nobles. "I told you," Donesha said. "I'd like my hair in spiral curls for the Christmas party," Milly said. "I'm not going to that party. You know that Hawaiian hussy's going to be there. If I were you, I wouldn't want to go either. She need to take her ass back on that island where she belongs."

"I don't care, I'm going. I haven't been to a party in a long time and I'm not letting some female stop me."

Larry was lying in bed wide awake. Kieha snuck in his room and got on top of him. "What are you doing?" he asked but with a smile.

"Trying to have some fun."

"I've told you many times, Kieha."

"Look we're adults."

"I know but I'm still not doing anything."

"This is just bullshit," Kieha said. She got up. "No swearing either."

Larry locked his door when he was finally alone again. He got comfortable in bed and thought about Milly Larry and Kieha checked four apartments in Johnson County Thursday morning. "The prices their asking for one bedrooms are way too much," he said, when they were riding back to Missouri. "We should stay in South Kansas City, or try in Midtown."

"Hell no! I heard it's ghetto, and the people out here aren't no better."

"Hold up, I know you're not trying to say something about my people. You're nobody to be belittling anybody."

"Are you getting smart with me?"

"No, I'm just telling you something."

"Well I don't need you tell me anything."

"What happened to you? You weren't like this when I met you."

Kieha just drove, refusing to listen to anymore. "I need to use the car."

"I need to get my eyebrows done," she said. "I'll drop you off," Larry said. "I'll only be an half an hour."

He dropped her off. Larry started to go by Arlene's, but he just phoned her instead. "Hey sis… do you by any chance have Milly's number?"

"Hello," Milly said. "Milly," Larry said. "Who's calling?"

"It's Larry."

"Larry… I'm surprised you're calling me."

"I want to come see you."

"Why?"

"I just want to."

"Larry, you have a lady."

"But we're friends. I can't see a friend?"

"Whatever your intentions are, I'm not about to get my feelings hurt."

Milly clicked over to call Donesha. "Larry just called me."

"Wow! Did he?"

"I didn't want him calling me because of that woman he got…I'm not feeling him anymore."

"How did he get your number?"

"I don't know. I thought maybe you gave it to him."

"No," Donesha said. "Arlene could of," Milly said. "Yeah. I have some great news…my kids are going to be in town today."

"Wow, that is some great news."

"This going to be one of the best Christmases in a long time."

"Yep, sure is," Milly said, sounding a little grumpy. Larry picked up Kieha and they went back home. Larry got out of the car. Kieha stayed in the driver's seat, with the car running. "You not getting out?"

"I have some running around to do."

"When will you be back?"

"Later."

She backed out the driveway and quickly drove away. Larry's mother, Agna was home. Her van was there. He thought she'd be knocked out sleep because she works overnight at the hospital as a nurse. She was up, waiting for him. "Mama why aren't you getting your rest?"

"I'm okay. I have something I really have to say to you."

"What is it?"

"I have a problem with that girlfriend of yours."

"What is she doing?"

"She leaves dirty dishes in the kitchen sink, when she eats, she leaves crumbs everywhere. This morning I found an empty douche bottle in the bathroom sink. I don't know who she thinks she is or where she thinks she's at…the Hilton or something. Ain't nobody here is her maid. Where's she from it's probably like that but here, I don't think so. That's probably why she's always gone so nobody can't make her clean up after herself. I don't see what you see in her stuck up spoiled bratty butt. And another thing… I don't understand why some of you black men want to go outside of your race."

"Come on mama you taught me race shouldn't matter."

"I know but some of you men get in trouble when you mess with any other race of women. What's the matter? You don't like sisters?"

"You know I love black women more than anything. You're a black woman and I love you."

"You should get yourself an independent black woman. I'm gonna get me some sleep now and Larry…I love you too. You've done a lot for me. I'm so glad you're here."

Three days 'til Christmas and look how it's turning out for me, Milly thought to herself while lying on her couch doing nothing, with the TV turned down low. *I have nobody in my life except my family. All I want to do is eat Christmas dinner and sleep for the rest of the day. Going to the party is out of the question. I'm not making my holiday more disturbing than what it is.* Kieha didn't come back until after eleven that night. Agna had already gone back to work. Larry was in the living room watching a watching a movie. "Where have you been?"

"Taking care of business," Kieha said. "I really have something to say to you. Why are you with me? You don't seem to respect me or anybody especially friends of mine. You're no better than anyone and because you don't think you have to tell me where or what you be doing…it's best you move out in the morning."

"You talking to me like this?" Kieha asked. "Who put you up to this? Your mother? I always knew you were a mama's boy."

"My mother has nothing to do with this. Why don't you leave right now? Since you want to keep sassing me."

"Fine with me it's your loss."

Milly woke up so early Friday morning, she decided to cook herself some breakfast. She looked at the calendar on her kitchen wall. *Today is December 23rd. I wish Christmas had already came* and gone. Milly went all out pancakes, bacon, cheese omelets, toast and some orange juice. She ate so little yesterday so she had to. Plus, this made her feel better. She's ready for the holidays to be over, she's ready to go back to work. That's all she's got going for herself. Milly gobbled all her food up. Her stomach was very satisfied. She went back to bed and slept for two hours. As soon as she got up, her cell phone rang. Milly was thinking it was her mother. She did not want to talk to nobody right now. It was an unfamiliar number, so she quickly answered. "Who's this?"

"Hi, it's Larry. Can we talk, please?"

"What about?"

"You have any plans today?"

"Not really."

"I wanted to see if you wanted to hang out?"

"Larry... "

"I know what you're thinking but I asked her to leave. I've really seen how disrespectful she's been. My mother has even brought it to my attention."

"You expect me to believe you're not with her anymore?"

"You don't have to believe me, but I'd like to meet you somewhere. You pick the time and place."

Milly had to think for a moment. *Should I or should I not. This is the man I've always dreamed about being with and now that I have the chance*—Crown Center," she blurted out. "Around two o'clock."

"Ok, I'm going to take the bus, so I'll meet you in the front," he said. "I'll see you," Milly said. "I guess this is going to be an alright Christmas after all," she said to herself.

Milly parked in the second level parking garage. She passed through the shops, went one level down the escalators and waited by the front where the information desk was. Milly looked at her cell phone. It was one forty-five. She was looking around at how crowded it was early in the day. Larry arrived within twenty minutes she's been standing there waiting. He gave her a hug. "I'm glad to see you."

"Me too," Milly said. "Have you been waiting long?"

"No."

"What do you want to do" Larry asked. "I don't know…we can find somewhere to talk."

"Also, something to eat. I'm hungry," he said. They found someplace to sit and got pizza. Larry was chowing down on his pizza. Milly was taking her time eating hers. "You're certainly not hungry."

"I had a big breakfast this morning."

"All I had was cereal. So, Miss Millian, you excited about Christmas?"

"No, not really."

"Why not?"

"I'm just not."

"Well I am. "Larry, what do you want?" Why are we here together?"

"Come on I'm not here with you to talk about her," he said. "She couldn't have just upped and went back to Hawaii that quick," she said. "Yeah, she left most of her stuff at my house, but I'm not involved with her anymore. She wasn't that way she is now when we were in Maui. That's the reason I brought her home with me because I thought she was the nicest girl I've dated in a long time. I guess you never really know anybody, but I know you Milly. I know you enough to see you're still that same girl from the sixth grade, just wanting a friend that will be there for you."

Milly and Larry talked for a while. Then they walked the mall, twice. It had gotten dark then colder outside. They even left together. "What are you getting into this evening?" Larry asked, as they were riding along. "I was just going to relax, see what good movies are on."

"You want some company?"

"Yes, sure."

"This is a cozy little apartment," Larry said, when they got to her place. "I love it here, it's so quiet. You want something to drink?"

"Yes."

Milly went to the kitchen. Larry sat down on the couch. She got some strawberry wine coolers out of the refrigerator. Milly picked up her TV remote and searched for something to watch. "What would you like to watch?"

"It don't matter. Whatever's on."

She settled for "Miracle On 34thStreet."

"I hope you like old movies. I've seen this movie a million times."

"It's a great movie," Larry said. Milly sat in her easy chair. "Why are you sitting over there?"

"This is my favorite chair."

"You'll be more comfortable on the couch."

"I don't know about that."

"We're known each other too long," Larry said. She gets out of her chair and sits on the couch. "What's your favorite movie?" he asked, "of all time?"

"I'll have to say the Wiz. I like the Wizard of Oz too, but Michael Jackson played a better scarecrow. "I really don't have a favorite."

Milly focused on the movie, Larry continued talking. "Let me know when you're ready to leave."

"You're ready to get rid of me? I wouldn't want to get rid of you."

"I wish that this moment, this whole day, was a dream," she said. "What are you talking about?"

"Larry, I have been so crazy about you for many years. I've fantasized about us being together. Now that we've spent time together, I can't believe it. This can't be real."

"Some dreams do come true," Larry said. "I thought about you a lot also." He touched her on the shoulder.

A warm feeling came upon her. "Maybe I should take you home now."

"Are you afraid of me or afraid of being hurt?"

"Both."

"What do you have to be afraid of? Milly, we've known each other almost our whole lives."

"But you've been away so long. The times you were around in town, I'd never seen you."

"You're seeing me now and I'm not going anywhere. I want to be your friend, Milly I mean we've always been friends but the friend you can count on. I'm here for you. I just hope you'll be here for me."

"Yeah, I would like to be that friend," Milly said. "Cool why don't we get something to eat."

"How about some Chinese?" she asked. "That's exactly what I had in mind."

They went out for thirty minutes and came back with some Chinese and some more wine coolers. They laughed, fed each other their shrimp and they went through the wine coolers. At one point, she noticed Larry staring with a smile on his face. Then he kissed her out of the blue. He was gentle about it at first but then he kissed her on the neck. She knew when his hand was going down on her, she was in trouble tonight. Milly brought Larry back home the next morning. "I had fun last night," Larry said. "Me too."

He gave her a big kiss. "You still coming to the party tomorrow night?"

"Yeah, I'm going shopping for something to wear."

"I know it's going to be sexy," he said, and gave her another kiss before he got out of the car and said, "I'll call you later."

Larry was about to get undressed, so he could take a shower, but someone was at the front door. "Well you here to pick up your stuff?" Larry asked Kieha. "Later. Right now, I just came for my coat, it's a lavender coat I need."

"You know where it's at?" he asked. "In the hallway closet."

Larry was about to go get it until she said, "Larry, are you going to let me in? It's cold out here."

He didn't want to, but he let her in. After she came in, they stared at each other. "I guess I have to get it. I wouldn't want you to break a nail," he said. Larry disappears. Kieha seen his cell phone laying on the couch. She gets some numbers from his phone before he returns. He hands her the coat and said, "be sure to call before you come by to get your stuff."

"Is that all you have to say?" she asked. "What?"

"You don't care about me anymore?"

"You got your coat, don't come back until you ready to get the rest of your stuff."

She puts her arms around him. "Come on, we've been together for two years. Remember those nights in Hawaii."

Larry pushed her away. "I'd appreciate it if you leave."

"You're just being like this because of that woman. I've been watching you, but you haven't seen the last of me! She jets out the door. Milly went to Donesha's house. "Go shopping with me today?" she asked Donesha. "I thought you were done with your Christmas shopping."

"No, I want to get something to wear to the party tomorrow. Another thing I want to ask…could you do my hair sometime today?"

"Sure, you're really trying to look extra cute for this party. I hope you're not trying to look good for Larry?"

"No, Larry likes me the way I am. Besides we're together now so I don't have to try."

"Wait a minute… you guys are together now? That doesn't make sense. So, he's dating you and the other woman?"

"He's not with her anymore."

"How do you know that?"

"I just know."

"What did you do, sleep with him?"

"Yeah."

"That's not a wise thing to do. I know you've always liked Larry and we both know he's nice guy but, something about this doesn't seem right. He's dated that woman for two years and brings her back home. What makes you think he has upped and dumped her?"

"He didn't break up with her just to get with me."

"I'm not saying he did."

"He said she was being disrespectful towards him and others. You should know that you saw how she acted when we first met her at Arlene's house."

"I know but you need to be careful."

"It seems like every time I get some kind of joy in my life everybody wants to take it from me."

"Don't look at it like that Milly. I care about you. You want to look pretty for this party, then let's get you prettied for this party. Donesha brought her two kids with her and Milly to the mall. It didn't take Milly long to pick out something and plus the place was too crowded, so she didn't want to keep them out too long. Before leaving the mall, a call came through on Milly's phone. "Milly?" the person asked. "Yes, who's this?"

"Kieha, Larry's girlfriend."

Milly stopped walking. "I advise you not to see him anymore. He's with me and he's always going to be with me. So, it's best you get over him."

Click, was what she heard after that. She was so shocked when she got off the phone, she stood still. "You alright Milly?" Donesha asked. Milly didn't respond.

Milly still wouldn't tell Donesha anything before she dropped her and her kids off at home. Donesha was so concerned about her, she called twice on her home phone but didn't reach her either times. Donesha notified Karla and they both went by there. They kept ringing her doorbell. Milly stayed away from the door and remained laid out on her couch, being very quiet. Karla took out her cell phone and tried calling her. She wouldn't get an answer. Milly's answering machine came on, so Karla left a message. "Millian… this your mother…I want to know…what is going on with you? I know you're in there. You shouldn't shut the world out because something is bothering you. We're here to help you."

Karla was hoping she would pick up the phone or open the door, but still silence. They went away but was really worried. Larry called an hour later. She wouldn't answer the phone even for him. He called back thirty minutes later.

Donesha ended up calling Larry. "Have you talked to Milly?" Donesha asked. "I just tried calling her. She's not answering," Larry said. "Are you guys dating?"

"We hung out yesterday."

"You're not seeing what's her face anymore?"

"No, I got sick of her attitude."

"Do you have any idea why Milly isn't speaking to anybody?" she asked. "No."

"She got a call while she and I were at the mall today. Ever since that phone call, Milly refuses to talk."

Larry tried to think who it might be. "It has to be Kieha. She came here earlier to pick up her coat. I left the room to get the coat for her and I think she went through my cell phone because I had it laying on the couch. I have something to take care of," he said.

Larry called Kieha.

"I want to talk to you."

"I'll be there in thirty minutes," Kieha said. "No, I'll come to you. You at home?"

"I'm out in Olathe shopping," she said. "Can you meet me in the town center parking lot in Leawood in thirty minutes?" he asked. "Yes, but where at in the parking lot?"

"In front of Macy's on 117thside."

"Larry, I knew you still cared about me."

Larry drove his mother's van to Leawood. He called Kieha when he got to Town Center, Macy's parking lot. She told him she was in the shoe department. It took him five minutes to find her. Kieha was trying on some high heels and there was some guy with her, sitting down. "Larry, I'm so glad to see you."

"Cut it out. You don't take phone numbers from my phone."

"Say what?"

"You heard me. Leave Milly alone. You need to hurry up and get the rest of your shit out of my house and don't even think about coming to the party either!" Kieha was heated after he left. Milly finally got off the couch after lying there for five hours. Larry came over. She stared at him with her door barely opened. "Let's talk," he said. "I really don't want to talk."

"Milly please."

She let him in and they sat down. Milly wasn't looking at him, but she could feel him looking at her. "So talk," she said. "I didn't lie to you. She went through my phone and saw your number."

"So, what are you going to do about her? I don't want to be involved with you if she's going to be causing problems."

"I've told her a thing or two," Larry said. "You think she's really going to listen to you?"

"Don't worry about her. She's not allowed to attend the party. I want you there. Did you ever get to pick out what you going to wear to the party? Arlene wanted everyone to wear red and white. But if you already got something else that's alright. My sister always like treating Christmas like Valentine's Day. It is the season to love. I know the place is going to be filled with mistletoes. I don't want you to be mad at me. I want you to be happy. It's Christmas Eve and I'll see you at the party tomorrow night."

Milly nodded her head. After Larry was gone, Milly looked at how many times her mother and Donesha had called on her caller ID. She went to the kitchen, opened up a bottle of Welch's sparkling grape juice that was sitting on the counter and poured some in a glass. She drank some then left the rest on the counter. She went to the bathroom. Milly looked at herself in the mirror and saw how wild her hair was. She thought to herself, *I need to do something to my head for the party.* "Oh no the party. I was going to have Donesha do my hair. It's too late. I was so out of it, I wasn't thinking about anything. I hope she can still do it," she said, dialing Donesha's number on her cell phone. "Goodness, Milly, are you alright?" Donesha asked, after Milly said who she was. "Yes, I'm fine. Are you able to still do my hair? I know it's late."

"I can still do it…it's not too late."

"Thanks, you're a real friend."

"I'll be there in twenty minutes," Donesha said Milly quickly washed her hair, conditioned it, and blow dried it before Donesha got there. She conditioned her scalp while Donesha plugged in the curling iron. She brought her son and daughter and they watched TV while their mom was doing Milly's hair. "I really appreciate this," Milly said when she finished conditioning her scalp. She sat down in a chair in front of Donesha. As Donesha was combing her hair, she still felt concerned about Milly. "Is everything alright with you?"

"Yes. Larry said not to worry about her."

"Her," Donesha said. "Larry was here not too long ago. He really wants me there at the party. Kia or whatever her name is not allowed at the party."

"Was that who you were upset over?" Donesha asked. "Yes, she got my number from Larry's cell phone when she came by his house to get something."

"Be careful. This woman sounds crazy. Bitch didn't want to speak but can look up numbers and say something over the phone," Donesha said. "What did she say to you?"

"To not see him anymore because she's with him and always will be."

"Yep, she's crazy alright," Donesha said. She spiral curled her hair up in thirty-five minutes. Milly went to her bedroom and got ten dollars out of her purse. She went to hand it to Donesha, but she refused to take it. "I didn't mind doing this."

"I don't mind paying you because you didn't have to."

Donesha took the ten dollars and hugged her It was about eight o'clock when Milly woke up called her mother and said, "Merry Christmas."

"Well Merry Christmas to you too. I'm glad you're doing alright. Donesha told me she talked to you yesterday evening."
"I couldn't be better."

"What time are you coming?" Karla asked.

"I'm getting ready now…so like in forty minutes."

"Yeah, hurry up and get your butt down here. Everybody's going to be here."

"I will. Milly rushed to the bathroom soon after she got off the phone. She was taking the rollers out of her hair. She wanted to make sure her curls stayed while sleeping in them. When she took the last roller out of her hair, she heard knocks at her front door. Milly *wondered who could this be at this time of morning?* She looked out the window and didn't see anyone. *Maybe it was the wind.* She headed towards her bedroom. She heard the knock again. She still didn't see anyone when she looked out the window again. Milly opened the door, poked her head out and looked around. *It's got to be the wind.* She shut the door and locked it. Next thing, the door knob was twisting like someone was trying to get in. Milly was frightened and confused. The doorknob stopped moving. She slowly unlocked the door and slowly turned the knob to open the door. The door flew open almost causing her to fall back. Kieha was staring at her fiercely in her own living room. "What the hell!" Milly yelled. "I really didn't want to do this, but I warned you to stay away from Lawrence."

"You don't come in my house and threaten me."

"Don't show up to that party," Kieha said. "He invited me and I'm going."

Kieha flared up. "Get out of my house before I call the police."

Kieha just stood there, looked more flared up. "That's it. I'm calling the police."

Milly was going for her phone sitting by the lamp. Her back was towards Kieha so she pulled out a crowbar from inside her coat and came closer to Milly. She raised it and screamed, "stay away from him!" She wacked Milly on the back of the head. She fell face forward. Kieha was shocked at what she done. She ran out and shut the door. She ran down the street and got into a car with a guy who was in the driver's seat. "Let's go!" she shouted. They drove away quick. Milly was unconscious, and the phone was off the hook.

Karla called Milly's house because it's been two hours since she's talked to her daughter. "No answer," she told Milly's father, Dan. "Let's go over there," he said. Milly had an ice pack on the back of her head. She was sitting on the couch, feeling furious. She was unconscious for about an hour. Milly was so mad she doesn't know what to do. The huge bump on her head was throbbing like hell and it gave her a headache. The door bell was rung. She wanted to tell whoever it was to go away or pretend she didn't hear the doorbell. "Milly, it's your mother!"

"Great," she said in aggravation. Milly wondered why both her parents were here after she opened the door. "What is going on here, Milly? You're not even dressed, and you look awful."

They all sat down. "I'm okay I fell asleep. I did have a hangover from drinking too much last night."

"Why you have an ice pack in your hand?" Karla asked. "I fell and hit my head."

"On what?" Dan asked. "A chair."

"Let me see where you hit your head."

Karla tries to touch her head but Milly scoots away. "It's nothing it will go away. I'll meet you at the house…I'm going to get ready now."

Karla and Dan stand up. "Don't be long Millian. Everybody's waiting on you."

"I'll be there in a flash."

The Starks family were having a Merry Christmas dinner and lots of fun. Milly couldn't enjoy herself for nothing. All she could think about her being hit in the head. That scared her. It could've given her brain damage or even killed her. Some of her family members knew something was up with her, but, didn't say anything. All she had on her mind was finding Kieha and getting her. *It's a damn shame what women would do to keep a man*, Milly thought to herself, "but she's not going to get away with what she's done to me."

Soon as Milly left her parents' house, she called Donesha. Donesha didn't answer but she called Milly back twenty minutes later. "Merry Christmas."

"Merry Christmas," Milly said back. "How's it going so far?" Donesha asked. "You were right, she's crazy."

"What is it?"

"Larry's supposedly ex-girlfriend attacked me."

"When? How?"

"This morning. She showed up at my front door just when I was about to go over to my parents' house. I told her to leave. She wouldn't leave so I turned my back on her to get to a phone, so I could call the police. Then out of nowhere she hit me on the back of my head with something hard. I've been having headaches."

"You should contact the police."

"I got to find out where she is, so they can go pick her ass up."

"How you going to do that?"

"It's a possibility she'll be at the party tonight."

"I'll go with you. Did you tell your parents what happened?"

"I didn't tell nobody. But she's gonna pay…everybody's going to know that."

Arlene's party started at seven. Milly didn't get dressed until after nine. Larry called her, but she didn't want to talk now. She wanted to show up at the party as late as possible to see who all was going to be there. She had no doubt in her mind Kieha was going to show up. Milly was brushing her hair. She had touched the bruised spot on the back of her head. It made her mad on how painful it was. She dropped her brush on the bathroom sink and was ready to go. Kieha had shown up at the party. Larry got upset when he opened the door to see her. "What do you want?"

"I wanted to come to the party. Your sister did invite me."

"But I told you not to come--- but since I'm here, could I?"

"Who's that Larry?" Arlene asked, coming through the crowd of people. Kieha inched her way in, walking toward Arlene. "Hi Arlene. Wow, your place is nice. I love all the decorations," she said, shaking her hand. Larry shut the front door and got on his cell phone.

Milly and Donesha arrived at Arlene's house at ten thirty. They were watching who all was showing up. "She might not show up," Donesha said. "She might show up or she could already be here. If only I knew what kind of ride she has."

Milly cell phone rang. "It's Larry," she said. "You still coming?"

"Yes, we're on our way right know. We should be pulling up in five minutes."

They conversated for a few minutes after Milly got off the phone with Larry, then they headed up to Arlene's house. Arlene had answered the door. "Alright, you gals made it."

"We weren't going to miss your party," Donesha said. Milly saw Larry before they came inside. She called his name.

When he was coming to her, Milly could've sworn she saw Kieha. She looked harder and Kieha realized Milly spotted her. Kieha tried to hide away in the crowd. Milly by passed Larry, eased her way through the crowd, came behind Kieha, and grabbed her. Kieha turned around and said, "don't touch me!" Milly pushed her, and she fell back. Kieha was sitting up on the floor screaming, "Larry!" because Milly was standing right over her looking like she was going to punch her. The people there didn't know what was going on. Larry came running over. "She's trying to attack me!" Kieha pointed at Milly and stood up. Milly pointed back and said, "I'm the one with the bump on my head bitch!"

"You shouldn't let crazy people near you," Kieha said to Larry. "Crazy!... I'll show you crazy!" Larry held Milly back. "Milly chill out."

"I'll chill out…for now. She hit me on the back of my head with…I believe with a crow bar or something…and I have evidence on me to prove it."

"I don't know what you're talking about. She could be on something," Kieha said. "I've known Milly forever. She's always been an honest person and has a good heart…you Kieha… you are full of it. You never had an honest bone in your body. You could of seriously injured her or even took her life."

Kieha held her head down. "Here's what you can do…you can apologize to Milly and mean it and never come around her again or get picked up by the police, what's it going to be?" Kieha sighed. "I'm sorry… it will never happen again." After saying that she left. "I don't think she meant it," Milly said. "Regardless if she meant it or not… she's not coming around here anymore," Larry said. "What a Christmas," Arlene said. "Come on everybody, let's continue to have fun, this is a party."

Milly came up to Arlene. "Sorry for all this."

"Don't be. I didn't like that help her anyway."

After Arlene walked away, Larry came up to her. "Doing alright?" he asked. "Yeah," answered. "Baby why didn't you tell me sooner?"

"I don't know… I thought you were still in love with her."

"I was never in love with her. I really liked her. I was a fool to even bring her back home. You want to dance?" he asked when a Luther Vandross Christmas song came on. They danced together on a few more songs until Milly said she was getting a little dizzy and was ready to go. "The night is still young," Larry said. "I know but I'd better go before you see me laying on the floor."

"I'll walk you to your car."

Milly told Donesha she was leaving. Donesha chose to stay and hoped she felt better. Larry walked her to her car. "You'll be all right driving home?"

"Of course, I don't have far to go."

Milly was about to get in her car when Larry asked, "Are you forgetting something?"

"What?"

"You didn't give me a kiss."

"Shame on me… how could I forget?"

It began to snow as they kissed. It was appropriate for this heated moment. The end.

ABOUT THE AUTHOR

Tamara Barnett, born in Longview, Texas 1976, a new author but has been writing for years. "Religion, Romance, and Real Life" (2017) was one of her first major books published and plans on publishing many more great books!